Timber's Fairy

Wolfsbane MC Book 1
Marissa Ann

I0589793

Credits:
Cover Design by: Francessca's PR & Designs
Editor: Rachel Goldman
Blurb Writer: Melissa Mitchell
ASIN: B07F2NN5LP   E-Book
ISBN-13: 978-0-692-15358-1

Author's Note:
I'd like to dedicate this book to my sweet daughter, Adamina. I hope and pray that one day you will find your prince even if he shows up on a Harley Davidson. You are destined for great things in this life. Keep reaching for your dreams and continue to write. Your stories and books are amazing!

I'd like to send a special thank you to my mom who has always been there with a shoulder to cry on or a helping hand when I was down. You have always been the greatest supporter of my dreams and I love you even more for that.

I'd also like to send a very special thank you to my best friend and editor, Rachel Goldman. We have been friends for a long time now and share a huge passion for books. We also have OCD when it comes to errors and misspelled words. Hopefully we got all that covered in this book. Thank you for pushing me to see my dreams to reality.

To my new friend and colleague, Nikki Bloom, thank you so much for all of your help. You and Francessca were amazing in always being there to help answer all of my crazy questions. I appreciate you both so very much.

CHAPTER 1

Mina

It was such a beautiful day today and I was glad I had decided to take a break from my computer to go have coffee with my best friend. Winter had been brutal this year with all the snow and ice. I didn't really mind the weather too much. It was one of the things that drew me to this area a year ago. Seeing the snow covered mountains off in the distance no matter what time of year, took my breath away.

"Morning, Bella!" I called out as I walked into the local coffee shop.

"Hey, Mina, I'm glad you are finally here. I can use a break! Find a seat. I'll get your usual and join you for a few minutes." Bella was one of the first few people to welcome me into their little community. She owned and operated *"Bella's Brew"*. Although we had only met 1 year ago, most people not from here mistook us for sisters. We were both slender, stood 5'4", straight black onyx hair with blue eyes and 25 years old. Some of the local townsfolk called us the Pixie sisters.

"So what's on your schedule today?" she said as she set our coffee down.

"I have a skype meeting with my editor later this afternoon but other than that there's just a long boring day of retyping corrections. Why? Did you finally decide you are ready to go get drinks with me later?"

"Yeah, I have. My Mom is driving me insane since she moved in with me. I will be SO glad when she can finally find her own place."

"So that's what it takes to get my BFF to go out with me. Move her 3 times divorced mother in with her."

"You are such a bitch some times." She said as we both laughed.

"Bella, I know it's hard but she's your mother. Surely she's not being that bad"

"Mina, I swear to God you have no idea! She did my laundry the other day although I have asked numerous times that she NOT go into my room. She did it anyway. Then when I got home she proceeded to inform me that it was really no wonder I was still a 25 year old single woman since I was still wearing what she referred to as granny panties!!"

"Bahahahaha! I am so sorry Bella but that shit is hilarious! Your mom is a total trip. I think she's fun to be around."

"Yeah, well, you are not the one that has to live with her. The breakfast crowd will be rolling in soon. You want to meet me here at around 7:00 and we'll go have drinks?"

Bella had no idea how much I envied her having her mom around. My parents had passed away 10 years ago leaving my oldest brother to raise a teenage girl. I checked my watch as I gathered my things to walk towards the door. "Sure, I'll see ya at 7. Hope the town is ready for the Pixie Sisters again!" Both of us were laughing as we remembered our last drunken night out.

******

I was late! Bella had already been texting my phone like crazy. I pulled up at *Bella's Brew* at 7:40. Bella of course was waiting for me at the front entrance and tried to climb into the front seat before I even come to a complete stop. I couldn't stop the giggle as I watched her struggle into my truck.

"I don't understand why in the world you have to have such a tall ass truck. Is it a *"Southern Thang"* as you like to say all the time? Or are you compensating for something?" She said with a smirk on her face.

"Ha-ha. Just shut up and get your seatbelt on so we can get on the road."

"Whatever! It's not like we aren't already late anyway. Bet you were so into your writing, you never looked at the clocked. They make alarm clocks for a reason ya know." She made it sound like she was put out by my lateness but the smile on her face told a different story.

"I know they do and that is precisely why I refuse to have one. I don't like distractions while I am working. And you know this already which is why I know you didn't actually start getting ready until 7:00."

"Yeah yeah, so where do we want to go tonight?"

"I thought maybe we would go over to *Blackcat Bar & Grill.* We can eat before we get good and started on those shots we love so much."

"I heard that some of the MC may be there tonight. They all came roaring through town earlier today. Blade, the vice president of the club, came in to get coffees for some of the guys. He mentioned it to me."

"Blade, huh? Anything you want to tell me about this guy?"

"No. Why would you ask that?" she asks with a hint of a blush to her cheeks and annoyance in her eyes.

"No reason. Forget I asked." I reply and decide to change the subject. "Kind of surprised we never ran into them ourselves last year the few times we went out for drinks. Do they ever get rowdy?"

"They don't usually hit up any of the local bars. They have their own private bar at their clubhouse. They only mix with the town on rare occasions. I only know of a few instances where the cops were called because of a bar fight. Those were probably over a woman. Who knows?" she said as she shrugged her shoulders.

We pulled up into the parking lot and noticed how filled up it was getting. There was a long row of bikes lined up outside. "Well let's go find a table if we can. Looks really crowded already."

We walked into the bar and spotted a table near the back wall. A look around the room showed that it really was crowded in here already. So I was surprised there was an open table. As soon as we sat down, a waitress I recognized started our way. Sara Blackcat was a sweet young girl. She was just barely old enough to serve the drinks in here. Her dad, Paul, had let her start working part time after she turned 21 last year.

"Hey, you two, been a few weeks since we've seen you in here. Do the two of you always synchronize with each other with what you are going to wear?"

Bella was wearing tight blue skinny jeans with a white halter top and black boots. I was wearing black skinny jeans with a red halter top and black boots.

"Yeah took a while to get Bella to go out again. Think our last night out scared her straight for bit. And the dressing alike is always unconsciously done."

"If you could remember that night Mina, it would probably have scared you straight too! And yeah the dressing alike is what got us talking to each other the first time she ever came into the coffee shop." Bella said while laughing.

"Hahaha. I remember it just fine and it really wasn't that bad!"

"Sara please remind her that threatening bodily harm to a man twice as big as she is while swinging a wooden chair drunk off her ass, IS that bad."

"Come on! He deserved it and you both know it. Besides, Paul got there before I managed to knock his head off anyway. Paul threw him out and told him to never come back. You can't touch a female without permission and think you can get away with it." I said trying to defend my actions.

"She has a point Bella. And we all know you didn't actually want him touching you."

"You tell her Sara! Now, how has school been going? Did you finally decide on a major?"

"Not exactly…" At the same time we all heard a loud whistle from across the room and turned in that direction. Apparently some of the motorcycle club needed drinks. "Tell me what you two will have. I need to go see what Timber and the club need."

"Just bring us two beers and two shots of vodka to start. And bring us both a plate of the spaghetti and meatballs with garlic bread. Thanks Hon'." I watched her walk towards the men on the other side of the room. They were all wearing cuts that said *Wolfsbane MC*. As I watched Sara take drink orders I noticed one of the men staring straight at me. It was too far away and too dark in the bar to get a good idea of what he looked like but I could tell he was a really built man. Although I couldn't see his eyes very well, I felt like a prey animal looking into the eyes of a predator.

****

Timber

The other guys in the club talked me into going to the local bar tonight. Everyone had been mostly cooped up inside for most of the snowy season. It was finally starting to warm up so that we could enjoy some much needed time on our bikes. Although we still rode in some snowy conditions, the snow around here was too much for anything other than a four wheel drive during winter.

We had been here for about an hour with me stuck in my head thinking over a new custom build we were working on. I didn't really want to come out tonight but my club enforcer, Snake, reminded me that the President of the club needed to party with the guys on occasion and not make everything about business. Snake leaned over and said, "Come on Prez, at least pay attention and stop thinking about that fucking custom!"

"Ha-ha, you know me so well. You know I can't help it. There's only one week left until the deadline for it to be finished."

"You know we will have it finished on time. We always do." Bear said. Bear was the club accountant. Although we were a 1% club, most of our business dealings were totally legal. When I took over after my old man passed away seven years ago, I put together a plan to get us almost completely legal in all aspects of our businesses. We still sold grass and really didn't plan on stopping from doing so. It was on its way to becoming legal anyway. Once it was legal in Montana we would get a license and continue on with business as usual.

"You all damn well know, Timber won't stop thinking until we deliver it next week. By then there will be a new custom order taking up his mind." My VP, Blade, said.

"Damn it, look what just walked in boys." Snake said to everyone at the table. I looked up and felt like I was punched in the gut as all the air left my body. I was looking at the most beautiful woman I had ever seen in my life. She was wearing tight black skinny jeans and a red halter top. Even though her and the girl that walked in with her looked so much alike they could be sisters, the one in the red got my blood pumping. I kept my eyes on her the whole time they walked across the bar to a table and while they talked with Paul's daughter Sara.

"That is two very fine ass women! Don't think I have seen the one in red around before." Bear said as he and everyone else at our table stared at the two women.

I looked to my VP with a raised brow. "Blade?"

"We all know the one in white, is Bella Winters. She owns *"Bella's Brew"* in town. The one in red is her best friend, Mina Star. She moved here a year ago. There isn't much information about her other than her being a writer and that she's from a small town in Mississippi. Her record is squeaky clean."

"How the hell do you always know all this shit Blade?" asked Bear.

"Because we have a damn good enforcer that finds out about anyone new in town and reports back his findings." We all chuckled at that. Our enforcer,

Snake was a wiz on a computer. He could find out just about anything he wanted to.

I continued to stare at Mina and decided I wanted to know more. We were low on beers so I whistled to get Sara's attention. Soon as she walked up I gave our orders. She went to fill them taking Mina and Bella their drinks and food first. When she returned to our table I decided to ask a few questions of my own.

"Sara, the two ladies in the back, Do you know them very well?"

"I've known Bella since I was in grade school. I met Mina when she moved here a last year. Why do you ask?" Now she was smirking at me. She knew exactly why I was asking.

Ignoring her smirk I asked "Does Mina come in here often?"

"Timber, if you want to know if the girl has a man, just straight out ask." She said while giggling at me. "The answer is no she doesn't. Neither one of them do. They hit it off with each other within days of Mina arriving in town and been best friends ever since. I haven't seen either one even go out on a date with a guy. If one of your boys asks Bella to dance though, tell them to behave themselves. Mina has a temper and will do whatever necessary to protect Bella and vice versa."

"What makes you say that?" Blade asked Sara. But Snake answered before she could.

"Last year one of the tourists was here drinking when the girls were. He grabbed Bella by the ass and Mina went nuts on him. She snatched up a chair and was about to hit him over the head. Paul came out of the back room just in time to save the fool from getting his head knocked off. Ha-ha, was the funniest shit I ever watched."

"You just watched that shit happen and didn't do anything?" Blade asks with anger in his voice. I briefly wondered what that was about.

"I took care of it." His smooth, calm answer told me all I needed to know.

"Good. Drink up boys. The night is still young." I say to all my brothers.

A round of "Hell, Yeah!" could be heard from around our tables.

Chapter 2

Mina

The bar had finally gotten so packed full of people that most had to stand up because there were not enough chairs. It looked like the entire town was out having a good time tonight. There was a lot of rowdiness and laughter from those within the MC. Over the last two hours I watched as their own number of people on that side of the room grew larger.

Most of the women that joined them definitely looked the part of what I would call biker bunnies. Those types of girls that hung around a motorcycle club hoping they'd catch the attention of one of the hot bikers and be made into an old lady. But they never realized that the type of attention they attracted was not the type that would help them to find a good man for more than one night.

I had asked Sara when she brought our food about the guy that kept staring at me. She said he was the president of the club and his name was Timberwolf although most people just called him Timber.

Bella and I were having a great time with our beers and shots. I decided it was finally time for us to work off some of the buzz we had going out on the dance floor.

"Come on girl! Getcha ass up and let's dance!!" speaking loud enough for Bella to hear me over the music and crowd.

"Lead the way, Pixie One!" Yeah maybe my best friend was a little bit more drunk than I was.

It was a fast rock song by the time we made it out onto the floor. There were so many people dancing already that there was barely any room. I was trying to not bump into anyone while I danced because that seemed to always bring on the wrong attention from men. They couldn't seem to realize that bumping into them accidentally didn't give them permission to grab hold of a lady without invitation.

About halfway through the song, I lost Bella in the crowd and figured she'd pop back up at my side soon as she realized I wasn't right next to her. The girl seriously couldn't hold her liquor.

As I moved and swayed my hips with my eyes closed, I felt two arms go around me. I jumped away like I was hit with a hot poker and turned around to give the guy a piece of my mind. He looked like a rich boy out trying to slum it with his other very rich friends. I had something against those who acted as if the world belonged to them.

"What the hell, I didn't ask you to dance with me! Don't touch me!" I said as he tried to grab me again.

"What the fuck is your problem? You think you too good to dance with me? Hell, I could probably buy a hundred bitches just like you. Should feel privileged I picked you out tonight." The rich bastard sounded as if he had a death wish. I was raised in the backwoods of Mississippi. We didn't take shit from anyone!

"You arrogant prick! There's not enough money in this world to get me to even look at you. Much less, dance with your slimy arms around me."

"You are a fucking bitch! I should show you how bitches like you get treated!"

About that time I felt heat at my back which made my body cover in chills. I knew without even turning around who it was. This was the same feeling I had earlier in the night while he stared at me from across the room.

"Is there a fucking problem here?" He said as he slid his massive arms around my waist pulling me into him. His voice was a deep growl like sound that made my female parts start to tingle.

You could see the rich slime ball deflate as he looked at the leather and patches Timber wore.

"Nah, there's no problem. I didn't realize she was part of your party."

"Now you know. So get to fucking walking before I teach you a lesson in how to treat a woman with respect."

We watched the slime ball walk away and then I finally stepped out of Timber's arms. When I turned around I had to look way up to see his eyes. He was easily 6 feet tall making me look like a shrimp next to his big muscular body. His hair was a deep dark brown that came to his shoulders and his eyes were almost silver in color that seemed to draw you in and see straight through. I realized we had been staring at each other for several minutes without saying anything.

"Um, thanks for that." Great Mina, you picked a wonderful time to be shy! "I'm Mina Star." I said as

I offered my hand. He grabbed it with his which swallowed up my small hand. Okay, girly bits are definitely sparking now. He still hadn't said anything back to me yet. "I guess I need to go find where my best friend ran off to."

"She was headed towards the lady's room. My name is Jaxson Creed but everyone calls me Timber."

"It's nice to meet you Timber. I'll go check on Bella." I said as I started towards where the restrooms were located. I kept thinking about Timber as I walked through the crowd. My body had never responded to a man just by him talking or shaking my hand before. I also wondered why he decided to come to my rescue like that and made me wonder what he could possibly want with me. With a past like mine, it was hard to trust that people, especially men, did things just to be kind.

****

Timber

I walked back through the crowd to the edge of the dance floor where I left Blade and Snake when I first seen that slimy bastard putting his hands on Mina. I didn't understand why I felt so much jealousy over a girl I didn't even know but I didn't really care to examine it in detail at the moment. Right now my mind was still on the tingle I felt in my arms from where I held her for the first time.

"The little bastard give you any trouble?" asked Snake.

"Of course not, He apparently knew enough about this area to recognize my cutt and what it meant. Although we make bank on these damn tourists coming into the area to rent cabins and shit, they are sometimes a lot of fucking trouble. Get someone to keep an eye on the rich pricks. I think they are the business party that rented a few cabins over at *Wolfs Ridge*."

"I'll call the prospects we have stationed over there." Snake said as he walked towards the door so he could place the call.

I watched as Mina and Bella came back through the bar from the restrooms. The girl was hot enough to make my blood turn to molten lava and I decided I'd find out just how hot it could burn.

"Think I finally found something or should I say someone to get my mind off that custom bike job." I said as my eyes ate her up from the top of her silky black head to the tips of those black boots.

"Ha-ha, yeah Prez, I think I see that you have. Let's go have a drink with the ladies." Blade said as we moved toward where the girls were sitting at a table in the back.

****

Mina

After I found Bella in the bathroom, supposedly touching up her makeup, I told her about the sleaze ball encounter and Timber coming to my rescue. Or rather, the rescue of sleaze ball because I can totally take care of myself! I made sure of that a couple years ago when I took self defense classes.

"I can't believe that I step away for only a few minutes and miss all the excitement!" Bella says as she sits back down at our table.

"That's all you care about girl? The excitement you missed? I want to know why you went sneaking off to the bathroom without saying a word to me about needing to go. What's up with that?" I narrow my eyes at her because I know something is going on. She has never just bounced off the dance floor and left me there without a single word.

"I don't know what you mean. I just needed to go and you were way ahead in the crowd already." She says looking everywhere but at me. Yeah something is going on with my best friend. I'm still looking at her, when her back straightens and her eyes get as big around as saucers as she looks over my shoulder. As I turn around to see what she's looking at, I realize that Timber and another guy from his crew are walking towards our table. I don't know who this other guy is but damn, is every guy in the *Wolfsbane MC* tall, muscular and hot as hell? Is that like in the requirements to join?

"Mind if Blade and I join you ladies? Promise we don't bite. Not yet, anyway." Timber says while looking straight at me. Bella of course starts her giggling.

"You should see your face Mina. You look like you are not sure if you want to "punch him in the throat" or eat him alive!" I rarely get embarrassed but I can feel my face heat up a little at Bella's comment.

"The saying is "throat punch 'em", not "punch him in the throat." I inform Bella as I continue to stare at Timber as he takes the seat closest to me.

"But isn't that the same thing, Mina? Good lord the way you talk sometimes in that twang, I wonder if we don't need passports to visit your hometown!" She says in reply while both guys just watch our conversation back and forth like they are watching a tennis match.

"No it does not mean the same thing girl! We have already talked about this. You still haven't caught on, ya never will. It's a "Southern thang". I reply making us both laugh.

"Are you sure you two are not sisters?" Blade asks.

"Nope." We reply at the same time and immediately cut up laughing again. I look over at Timber and he's just watching me. As if he is trying to figure out exactly how to take me.

"Where are you from? That accent is very unique. Can certainly tell it's Southern but which State?" Timber asks me.

"I am from a very small town in North Mississippi."

"Why did you move to Montana?"

"Are we playing hundred questions now?" I ask with a raised brow.

"Just small talk darlin'. What made you want to move way out here?" he persisted.

"Well, after college I decided to do some traveling. I always wanted to see more than just what could be found in our small little town. Don't get me wrong, I love it there but not enough to really feel like I was at home. I had been traveling for about a year, never staying longer than a week in any one place, when I came through White Summer and rented a cabin at *Wolf's Ridge*. While staying there, I took short drives around a lot of the mountain roads. On one of those drives I spotted a beautiful cabin that was posted for sale. It was rustic, needed some work but the views were breathtaking. A month later I finally contacted the realtor about buying it. So now, here I am."

"So you stayed at *Wolf's Ridge*? Surprised we didn't run into each other. Our MC owns and operates the place. A year ago would have been right after all the upgrades we put into it. Did you enjoy your stay while there?"

"Yes, it was a very nice place. I was actually very surprised at the low cost of the rentals compared to how nice it was, including the buffet bar."

"So what does your family think about you moving way off into the wilds of Montana?"

"My brothers still are not taking it very well. After our parents died when I was 15, both of my brothers stepped up to take care of me. And boy have they taken the role of parent seriously."

"Hey guys, Bella and I are going to hit the dance floor." Blade says catching our attention that our friends are already standing up from their chairs.

"We'll join you." Timber replies as he helps me from my chair like a regular every day gentleman.

****

Timber

I wasn't acting myself and I knew it. Hell even Blade knew it. He kept giving me the side eye like he expected me to grow two heads and speak in tongues. Just something about this girl had me acting all kinds of wrong in a good guy kind of way. But I wasn't a good guy. I was a wolf in sheep's clothing, maybe. I had so much blood on my hands from my past, I was afraid to even touch this girl. She was tough, sure, but still just a good girl.

I didn't go for the good girls. They were not normally my type. They had expectations, wanted relationships and eventually marriage. I was used to the biker bunnies that I didn't have to care about getting dirty or forming hurtful attachments to me. They knew what was up from the get go. This girl was definitely going to be trouble. But fuck all if I cared right this moment.

We got to the middle of the dance floor and I pulled her into my arms. Again that tingling sensation was back and it was making my dick hard as hell. She had her head laid on my chest and I could smell her sweet scent. She smelled like tropical fruit which did not help the tightness in my jeans one damn bit but no way in hell was I letting her go now that she was in my arms. But there was no way she didn't know how I was reacting to her.

We were on our third slow song, because yeah I signaled to the DJ to keep that shit slow, when Snake showed up next to me.

"There is something that needs your immediate attention Prez." Giving me a look that told me I was not going to like what he had to tell me.

"I'll meet you outside in 15 minutes. Round up the rest of the boys." He nodded once and walked off. I turned back to Mina, "Are you and Bella staying longer?"

"Nah, it's late and I think I need to get her home. She doesn't hold her liquor too well." She said looking over at Bella who looked more like she was asleep in Blade's arms than dancing.

"Are you okay to drive you both home?"

She nodded with a smile "Yeah, I'm good. I knew I would need to drive so I stopped having shots way before Bella did."

"We will walk you out then." I signaled to Blade we were heading to the door. He swung Bella up into his arms and just carried her. He grinned at me as I watched him. The man knew how to play the gentleman far better than any of the rest of us in the club.

Outside we walked the girls to a newer model 4 door, 4-wheel drive Dodge Ram. It looked like she had a lift kit on it and it made me wonder how the two little pixies could even get up into the damn thing. Blade walked around to the passenger side and helped Bella into the seat. I could tell he was talking quietly to her while he also helped her with her seatbelt.

I opened the driver side door and took Mina by the hand to help her up. Just before she stepped up into the cab, I pulled her back and into me. She was looking at me with a question in her eyes.

"I got to have just one taste before you go Mina."

"Just one?" She asked quietly.

"For now…" I growled as I slammed my mouth onto hers causing her to tense up. The second my tongue slid along her bottom lip, she relaxed and let out a sigh as she opened for me. My first taste of her sent a shot of white hot liquid fire straight to my cock. I couldn't stop myself from sliding my hands down to her ass and pulling her up into me even closer causing her to moan into my mouth. This girl was truly an innocent and it showed in the way she was kissing me back. It made me want her even more.

I slowly pulled away from the kiss looking into her lust filled eyes as I lifted her straight into the driver side seat. "I will see you again real soon. Drive carefully." I said as I shut her door and walked back towards my brothers.

"Tell me." I said to Snake as Blade and I watched the girls drive away.

"Someone blew the lock at the bike shop and trashed the place."

"What about the custom we've been working on?" asked Blade.

"It was knocked over. The paint job will definitely need to be redone on the gas tank. Tires were slashed so those will need replaced as well."

"*DAMN IT!?!*" I was so pissed off I needed to calm myself. I needed a target for my anger but didn't want that target to be one of my brothers. "What else?"

"It doesn't look like anything was taken and they didn't even try to hack into the main computer as far as I can tell at the moment from my phone. They definitely wreaked the place, smashed a couple of the computers and pushed all the shelves over."

"Tell me we know who the fuck did this."

"Not yet we don't. Appears from the video feed there was only one person, all dressed in black with a mask. Soon as we get back to the clubhouse I will go through the feed slowly and see if I can get anything useful. We haven't had any run-ins with anyone since going legit. So this break-in doesn't make a hell of a lot of sense."

"Who the hell knows? It could be someone from our past looking to start trouble. Let's get back to the club and see what we have." I turned to Blade and said, "Call in all the guys, emergency church in an hour."

We all climbed on our bikes and took off towards the club to figure this shit out. We might be almost completely legal but we were still a 1% club. We would handle business one way or another. In this life, you live by the gun and you died by the gun.

****

Chapter 3

Mina

On Sunday morning I was out on my porch drinking coffee trying to keep my thoughts on my new book. There didn't seem to be anything that could distract me very long though from the memory of kissing Timber two nights ago. I had never been that attracted to a man before and I had certainly never had these types of feelings. Just the thought of his kiss caused my thighs to squeeze together and my panties to become wet.

Ever since the encounter with my ex-boyfriend the night of my 21st birthday party I had made sure to never allow another guy to get that close to me. Not even those I considered family. But for some reason I didn't feel anxiety when Timber held me. I felt protected and safe. Kind of a contradiction when you looked at how solidly built the man was. He should have frightened me with how big he was and how intense his gaze could be.

My thoughts were interrupted when the phone rang. Just by the ring tone I knew it was my brother, Rafael. I had been avoiding his and Mathis' phone calls since our last argument. They both took the parent role way too far and were having a hard time learning to let me live my own life.

I decide I should probably answer the phone before they decide to come out for a surprise visit. "Hey, Rafe."

"Do not hey, Rafe, me. Why the hell have you not been answering your phone? I understand that you have been pissed off at the two of us but that is no reason to make us worry about you."

"You and Matt need to learn to stay out of my business and let me live my life. I am not a teenager any more. You had no right to pay off the loan on my cabin! I told the both of you before and I'll say it again. I make plenty of money to pay my bills. I do not need y'all's money. I'm doing well here and want to make my own way."

I can hear him take a deep breath and sigh on the other end of the phone. The frustration he feels is clearly in his voice. But I am not a kid that needs to be taken care of any more.

"Mina, we just want you to never go without. To always be happy. We are just doing our part to ensure that. When mom and dad died, we swore we would always make sure that you were safe and well provided for."

"I understand where you are coming from, Rafe, but you need to understand where I am coming from as well." I say to him gently. I love my brothers and don't want them to feel like I don't appreciate everything they have done for me.

"How about I promise you that we will try? Do you forgive us now?"

"Yeah, I guess so." I say with a smile. "Where is Matt anyway? He's usually on the line with you."

"He's out on a run for the club. So what you been up to lately? Have you and the other little pixie been hanging out?" He asks.

I roll my eyes. I should have never told him about Bella and I being nicknamed Pixie One and Pixie Two. "We went out to *Blackcat* on Friday night for drinks." My mind immediately went to thoughts of Timber.

"Um hmm, did something happen? Your voice did that squeaky thing it does when you have something you don't want me to know. Care to go ahead and share?"

"My voice does not get squeaky!" feeling offended about his comment.

"Ha-ha, yeah it does kiddo. Now stop stalling, just spit it out. Might as well tell me now, you know I will find out anyway."

"And one of these days dear brother I will find out how exactly you know what I am doing. I swear if you have a prospect out here spying on me, you will not like what I do!"

"I promise we have not sent anyone to spy on you. When you left, you said that you didn't want the MC to follow you, that you needed space from us. As much as that hurt, we kept our promise to stay away but you promised to stay in touch with Matt and me. Don't shut us completely out of your life, *Fairy*." He said, calling me by the nickname given to me by the club brothers when I was younger. "Matt and I would like to come for a visit when you feel up to it."

"You think you can come for a visit without most of the club coming along with you?" I say on a laugh.

"Ha-ha, you are right. But we all would like to come visit, soon as you are ready to let us back in. We miss you, we all do. Hang on a minute." I heard someone talking to Rafe in the background while I waited for him to come back on the line. The voice was too muffled for me to figure out who it was. "I need to go sweet pea. I'll call you again in a few days. Maybe by then you will be ready to tell me about your night out. Love you little Fairy."

"Love you too, Rafe." I said as he hung up the phone.

His words kept playing back through my head. I knew they all missed me but I still wasn't ready to allow them back into my life. They still hadn't learned yet to stop trying to control everything. Having an entire MC full of overbearing protective men was enough to drive any girl insane. There had only ever been one boyfriend they couldn't run off from my life until the night he tried to hurt me. He got lucky they didn't kill him. Instead they gave him a solid beating and I hadn't seen him since.

****

Timber

I left out for an early morning ride. The fresh air and open road always helped to clear my head. We hadn't yet gotten a lead on who had broken into the bike shop or what they may have been looking for. As I was coming through town I noticed Blade's bike parked outside of Bella's Brew and decided I'd stop to grab my own cup of coffee this morning. I could see him through the window at the counter talking to Bella as I parked. I never did get a chance to ask him what he was talking to Bella about the other night so intensely. The bell above the door announced my entrance and they both turned towards the door.

"Good morning Bella." I said as I gave Blade a chin lift.

"Morning." She said softly looking at Blade before looking back at me. "What can I get for you Timber?"

"Just a black coffee will do." I head towards a table in the back. As I take a seat, Blade sits at the chair across from me. "What exactly are you up to Blade?"

"Nothing, Don't worry about it."

"Are you sure? You and Bella seemed really close on Friday night and now I find you in here on a Sunday. You can't claim you are here for coffees for all the guys since the shop is closed today."

"I said its nothing. Just leave it alone." He's my best friend and I can tell he's bothered by something but I don't push the issue. He'll talk when he's ready to but not before. So I change the subject.

"Has Snake been able to find anything else on the security feed?"

"Not yet. He said soon as he did he'd give us both a call."

"Hope he finds something soon. I hate all this damn waiting around. If trouble is coming our way, I'd damn sure like to know ahead of time."

"You got that right." He says as Bella sets our coffees in front of us.

Before she can walk away I ask, "Your friend, Mina, seems like a pretty great girl. Do you know anything about her life before she moved here?"

"Timber, she is my best friend and I will not give away all her secrets to you. If you want to know about her, you will have to ask. I will tell you though that she has major trust issues, especially when it comes to guys. I'm not even sure why. I suspect she has kept a lot more to herself than she's even told me. She doesn't talk about her family much or about her life before she moved here. I can give you her phone number before you leave if you want."

"That would be great Bella, thank you." I say as she walks back towards the counter as another customer comes in.

Blade and I stayed a while longer talking about the custom bike jobs we had coming up. As the lunch crowd started to trickle in, we left. We tried not to mingle too often with the people around town. Most were afraid and would cross a street just so they wouldn't have to walk close to any of us. There were a few like Bella that treated us like we were normal citizens. She had handed me a piece of paper with Mina's number on it as I was leaving.

When I got back to the club house, I grabbed a beer from the bar and headed to my room. I lay back on my bed and grabbed my phone to send Mina a text. I wanted to see her again although I knew I probably shouldn't. I could tell during our kiss that she was innocent. Those types of women had never attracted me before. I could also tell she was full of secrets and probably hiding something. But I didn't care. I had decided Friday night that I wanted this girl and I was definitely going to have her.

****

Mina

Around lunch time I decided to take a break and eat something. I was stuck on a specific love scene for my book that had kept my mind thinking about Timber. Lord, that man had my mind so preoccupied. I was coming up on my deadline and needed to get this book finished. Instead I was driving myself crazy thinking about a pair of calloused hands attached to thick tattooed arms and a pair of silver colored eyes.

I was on the porch eating a sandwich when I heard my phone ping with a text message. I picked it up noticing it was from an unknown number but figured I'd better check it just in case it was from my editor. She had a habit of texting me from any phone she could get her hands on. When I opened it, there was a picture of me from Friday night when Timber was holding me on the dance floor. You could tell it was taken from a good distance but it was definitely me. The text with the picture just said *"I see you."* This made me scan my surroundings and get an uneasy feeling as if someone was watching me.

Inside the house I quickly locked all the doors and checked my windows. As I moved a curtain aside in the living room to look back outside my phone pinged again. It was another unknown number. When I opened it I could tell it was from Timber and quickly forgot about the weird text message with the picture.

Timber
"I enjoyed Friday night and want to see you again."

Mina

"What did you have in mind?'
Timber
"Go for a ride with me. I can pick you up around 5?"
Mina
"I'll be ready at 5 ;)"
Timber
"I'll see ya soon."

The clock on the wall said it was 2:00 so that gave me three hours to pick out an outfit and get ready for my date with Timber. Was it a date? If it was a date, why did I so readily say yes when I hadn't given any other man the time of day in years? This man really did have my brain running in circles. Just what are you thinking Mina? I asked myself as I went towards my bedroom to start getting ready.

I had just gotten out of the shower when I heard my phone ringing with the tone specifically for Bella and I ran to the other room to grab it before she could hang up.

"Hello chica! Whatcha know good?"

"Seriously Mina, I am going to need you to write a book just so I know all these crazy sayings of yours. I am calling to let you know that I gave Timber your phone number today. He and Blade were here for coffee this morning. I got swamped with the lunch crowd and wasn't able to call you earlier."

"I figured you were the one to give it to him. He sent me a text a little while ago to see if I wanted to go out for a ride with him."

"Did you say yes?" she asks with a giggle.

"Yes, I did. He's supposed to be here at 5 to pick me up. I just got out of the shower and I have no idea what I am going to wear. Did he say anything else when he got my phone number from you?"

"Not really. He just asked about your life before you moved here. I told him that if he wanted to know anything that he'd best ask you. Anything that I personally know, I wouldn't tell if he paid me to. You are my best friend and I wouldn't betray you."

"Okay. Thanks Bella. I guess I should finish getting ready. I'll call you later."

"Have fun tonight Mina!" I hang up and head towards my closet hoping I can find something worth wearing.

****

Timber

As I was headed out of the clubhouse at 4:30, Snake was crossing our parking lot towards me. "Hey, I wanted to let you know that I found something on the video footage from Friday night. I was able to clear up the picture and get a partial of a tattoo on the guy's neck."

"Do you know what it is yet?"

"Not yet but I made some calls to some tattoo artists we know and sent them a picture to see if any of them has ever seen one. Hopefully they will get back in touch with me soon."

"Just let me know when they do. I am headed out for a while but I will be back later for church. We have to make sure we are on schedule for everything coming up this week."

"Are you going to see that hot little piece from Friday night?" He asks causing me to fight to control my anger.

"Watch it Snake, her name is Mina. I will be bringing her with me later and I suggest every one of the brothers keep a civil tongue or I will *cut it out*." I growl out giving a reminder of just what I am really capable of.

He throws his hands up and starts backing away from me. "I didn't mean any disrespect, Prez." His eyes wide and watching me closely.

I breathe slowly, relaxing my hands where they curled into fists, trying to let all the anger completely go that rushed over me so quickly. Jealousy was a bitch and I absolutely hated that it caused me to overreact to one of my brothers. These men were my only family. I trusted them with my life and knew that they would never step out of line where Mina was concerned.

"Sorry man, I'm just under a lot of pressure right now with everything." I say as a way of easing the tension.

"Yeah, we can blame it on everything going on if you want, but only if that pressure is ugly, green and in your jeans!" He laughs as he turns towards the door.

Chapter 4

Mina

I was ready to go way earlier than I needed to be. My nervousness was off the charts so I decided to work some more on my book. I was so lost in my work I jumped almost out of my skin when there was a loud knock at my door. I swung the door open to see Timber leaning on the door frame. He was in fitted blue jeans that had rips at the knees and a black t-shirt that his muscles made look like the shirt was entirely too small for him along with his leather cutt. He looked delicious.

"Hey, are you ready?" He said. I looked towards the clock on the wall and realized it was 5 already.

"I didn't even realize it was close to time. I get so caught up in my writing that time seems to pass me by without even realizing. Let me grab a jacket and we can go." I grabbed my jacket off the back of my couch and we walk out to his bike.

"Have you ever ridden before?" he asks.

"I used to ride with my brothers every chance I got." I immediately stop talking as soon as I realize what I said.

"Oh, so your brothers ride?" he says while looking at me. I shake my head. I know he expects more of an answer but I am not ready to spill that can of worms just yet. No one back home really understands why I left or why I cut them almost completely from my life. Even I'm starting to question why I did it. It's not like they were mean to me or anything. All the guys in the club treated me like a sister. They weren't the ones that broke me.

"So where are we going?" I ask as I climb onto the back of the bike and put the helmet he hands me on.

"I thought we'd drive the mountain roads for a bit. I got to meet with my guys around 7 at the clubhouse but figured you could come with me. We can have a few drinks in the bar there while we talk."

"Sounds good to me." I say as he starts up the bike and we head out.

To finally get to see these beautiful mountains I fell in love with from the back of a bike was better than I ever imagined. I had always loved the way it felt to ride the open road. The wind blowing through my hair and the growl of the bike is like nothing you can ever truly describe.

I had my own bike back home. Its one of the things I missed the most besides my family. The day Matt and Rafe surprised me with it was one of the best and worst days of my life. My 21st birthday should have been one of my best memories. They had surprised me with it when I first got up that morning. I spent most of the day riding, but after that night, I never could get on my bike without thinking about Josh holding me down on the floor of that shed.

After riding for a bit, we slowed down and pulled through a gate. We parked in front of a plain building and I knew it was his clubhouse. It wasn't much different from the one I was used to back home.

We climbed off the bike and Timber threaded his hand through mine. It made me feel good. I still couldn't figure out why or how being with this man made me feel so safe. I felt like I could breathe again after feeling like I had been holding my breath for the past 4 years.

We walked into the main room which was also a bar. There were several members sitting around tables, some were playing pool in the back. They all looked up as we walked in. And the one I recognized as Blade walked towards us.

"Nice to see ya again, Mina." He said giving me a smile and turning towards Timber. "All the guys are here."

"Okay, everyone head on back to the meeting room. I'll be there in a few minutes. I'm going to get Mina comfortable at the bar first." Timber says as he leads me towards one of the bar stools.

"Hey Fang, get Mina here whatever she wants. We are going into church so we'll be a little while. Keep an eye on her."

"No problem Prez." Fang says and then turns and asks me, "What will you drink pretty lady."

"A beer will do Fang. Thank you." I answer. I look back at Timber, "Do you think it'll take a while?" I ask.

"Hopefully, it won't take too long. Just stay right here and don't wonder off until I come to get you." He says smiling at me.

"Okay." And he kisses the top of my head before walking towards the hallway most of the other guys went down. I turn back to the bar and start drinking my beer.

I had been sitting at the bar for about 30 minutes when one of the biker bunnies sat on the stool next to me. Fang looked over at her and gave her a hard stare.

"What do you want Vivi?" He asks her.

"I'll have a beer." She says in the most annoying voice I think I have ever heard. It's almost like she's talking through her nose. After Fang turns to get her a beer, she turns on her stool toward me. "I saw you walk in with Timber. What? Looking for a walk on the wrong side of town? From the look of your expensive clothes you are clearly in the wrong place." She says with a curl to her lip.

"Vivi, I'd suggest you get your skank ass back across the room and wait for Bear. Mina belongs to the Prez. You go fucking with her and he's likely to throw your ass out." Fang says while leaning close across the bar.

"Whatever, we know her type can't hold a man like Timber. She'll be old news next week." She huffs as she gets off the stool and walks away. I raise my eyebrow and look to Fang.

"Should I be worried about anything?" I ask him.

"Nah, she's just another yote that's been after Timber since she showed up 6 months ago. The Prez has never touched her no matter how hard she's tried. Bear seems to be the only one to play with that merry go round." He says causing me to laugh out loud. "Want another beer while you wait?"

"Another beer would be good. What exactly is a yote?" I ask while taking a sip of my beer.

"That's what we call the hang-arounds like Vivi. It's short for coyote." His explanation causing me to suck beer down the wrong way and I start coughing while laughing as well.

"Seriously? Is that supposed to be some sort of "Coyote Ugly" reference?", still laughing hysterically. Fang starts laughing with me.

"You have to admit that shit is pretty fucking funny." He says when we both calm down enough from laughing so hard.

My phone goes off with another text message. I dig it out of my pocket and notice it's from the same unknown number from this morning. My heart starts racing as I open up the message and read the text. "*You are still just as beautiful as I remember. Soon we will be together again.*" The text gave me the chills. It also worried me. I didn't know who the hell could be doing this. I looked around the club but know whoever it is can't be here. I don't really know any of these people.

"Are you okay Mina?" Fang asks me.

"Yeah, yeah, I'm fine." I answer as I lift my beer and finish it off.

****

Timber

We all get settled around the table in the meeting room and I wait for my men to settle down before I start.

"We have that new shipment of weed that needs to go out on Thursday. The trucks need to be loaded and on the road by 3am."

"I have already made all the arrangements. Our guys should meet up with our contact 2 hours south of us at the warehouse on time." asks Butcher, our Road Captain.

"Good, on to other business. Where are we at on the custom that's supposed to be picked up on Tuesday? Will it be ready to go or do I need to see about buying us a day or two?" I ask while still feeling frustrated with the fact someone came into our shop and tried to destroy thousands of dollars worth of bikes, parts, and tools.

"Since we didn't take the weekend off because of the damage from the break-in, we should be able to finish it up just before time for the guy to pick it up. I'd like to know who the mother fucker is and take my time drawing out some medieval torture practices." says Blood, our sergeant at arms. We all knew he was into the more gruesome aspects when it came to getting rid of those that would cause issues for our club. We all may have cleaned up our image as best we could but none of us forgot who we were deep inside.

"Snake, you want to share with the brothers what you found?"

"I was able to go through all the video feeds slowly and finally got a picture that may can help us with identifying who he is." he says as he passes out pictures for the other brothers to see. "I also sent copies of these to all the tattoo shops where we have connections. I am hoping one of them may have seen this tattoo before and can give us more to go on."

"Snake you continue to see what you can find. Let us know soon as you do. Blade, contact the guy about the custom and let him know it can be picked up at 7pm Tuesday night. Butcher, you and Blood, make sure everything is ready for the weed shipment on Thursday." I say as I end our meeting.

I leave the room going back into the bar and spot Mina where I had left her on the stool. As I walk up I hear Fang ask her if she is okay and her saying yeah but she then picks up her beer and chugs it back like someone finding water in the desert. As I come up behind her, I slip my arm around her.

"Hey. Did you finish your meeting?" she asks.

"Yeah, all finished for the night. You ready to go?"

"Yes but I need to use the restroom first."

"It's just down the hall on the right." I answer, pointing her in the right direction. I take a seat on the stool she just vacated and watch her walk down the hall.

"Boss, I thought I should let you know that Vivi came up to her while you were in church. She told your girl that she wouldn't last long around here."

"That bitch is pushing my restraint. What did Mina say?"

"She asked if she should be worried and I told her no. I told her you had never been with Vivi although she's been trying ever since she first came here."

"Good, I don't want anything coming between her and me."

"You really like this one." He states with true surprise on his face.

"This one is going to stick." I say as I watch Mina come back down the hall. "You ready to go baby? I thought we could pick up something to eat on our way back to your house if that's okay with you." I say to her.

"That sounds really good. What did you want to eat?"

"Do you like Chinese food? I know they are still open and they won't take long to put together a to-go order."

"Chinese would be perfect. I've been living on sandwiches lately, so I haven't had a good hot meal in a while."

"Let me guess, it's because you get lost in your writing?" I say with a chuckle causing her to smile. "Come on, let's go."

When we pulled up to her house, she helped me to get all the food out of my saddle bags and we took it into her house. I had been in this cabin a few times back when it belonged to the previous owners. She clearly had done a bit of work on the inside. While it was simple, she had painted the inside bright colors that made the rooms seem bigger than they actually were.

"I like what you've done to the inside." I state as she pulls down plates and glasses for us.

"Thanks. I didn't do too much to it when I moved in. Paint goes a long way to making something look better."

We both sit down at the table and as we begin to fill our plates, her phone rings. She grabs it up and just looks at it. "Are you going to answer it?" I ask.

"It's just my brother Matt. I can call him back." She says as she rejects the call. But not even a minute later, it starts ringing again.

"It doesn't look like he wants to wait for a call back. It could be important. Go ahead and answer it."

"Okay, I'll be back in a few minutes." She says as she walks out the door to her back deck.

I don't mean to listen in on her conversation but she didn't shut the door all the way. As I listen, I am filled with even more questions that I am sure she will not be willing to answer.

****

49

Mina

I leave Timber in the kitchen while I step out onto the back deck through the sliding glass door. Rafe must have told Matt that I had finally answered the phone and decided to check in with me himself since he hadn't been present for the call with Rafe.

"Hello."

"There's our Fairy! It's about damn time for you to forgive us and start answering your phone." He grumbled over the line. I could hear music in the background and muted voices.

"Rafe already gave me an ear full about not answering the phone. So you can save it. I don't need another lecture. Are you at the club? I hear music."

"Yeah, we had a BBQ earlier with everyone here. Everyone has been asking when you might allow us to start visiting. You've been gone a long time."

"I know it's been a long time. I miss all of the brothers too, especially you and Rafe. But I'm still not ready just yet." I say with hesitation in my voice.

"Why? This is getting ridiculous! We have given you more than enough time and space to get your head back on straight. Look, we know that what happened broke something inside of you that night. Hell, everyone could see it that entire two years before you left. You never allowed yourself to be alone with any of the brothers. While that hurt them, we all understood it." his words causing tears to gather in my eyes.

"No Matt, I don't think *any* of you can understand how I felt. I had never felt that vulnerable before. I lived in a damn bubble thinking I was safe, that I would always be safe because I had all of you. But it winded up being one of you that made me afraid of the world around me. I *HAD* to leave or I thought I'd go crazy. I'm just now starting to feel like my old self again."

"Okay little Fairy, just calm down. We will stop pushing so hard, at least for now. So tell me what you have been up to? Have you made any friends?"

Him asking if I made any friends caused me to turn around and look through the glass to see Timber still at the table eating. "I made a few." I answer quietly.

"Well tell me his name." Matt asks on a chuckle.

"Exactly how do you know there is a he?" I demand as I watch Timber look up and straight at me through the door.

"Come on, Fairy, It's in the way you said it. So who is he?"

"I gotta go Mathis."

"You seriously won't tell your favorite brother?"

"Uh huh, I will not fall for that! You will run back and tell Rafe that I said you were my favorite!" I say while laughing.

"But I am your favorite!"

"I love you Matt but really, I got to go."

"I love you too little Fairy. Call us if you need anything."

"I will, I promise." I say before hanging up the phone with him.

When I return to the kitchen, Timber is sitting back in his chair just looking at me.

"Is something wrong?" I ask. But he continues to just look at me before he returns to his plate.

"You're food is getting cold. You may need to reheat it." He says.

I grab my plate and after I've reheated it in the microwave, I sit back down at the table. Timber continues to eat and seems to be avoiding looking at me. After we have finished, I get all the food put away and load the dishwasher.

"Is something wrong, Timber?" I finally ask him.

"Nothing is wrong but I need to get back to the clubhouse soon. I have an early morning tomorrow with the crew in the shop."

"I'll walk you out." I say walking towards the door.

We step out onto the porch and he turns to look at me. His silver colored eyes seem to penetrate me and cause my nipples to tingle. Just one look and this man has me turned on like no other ever has.

He reaches out and grabs me by my hips and slowly pulls me to him. When my chest meets his, I can't stop the low moan in my throat from escaping. He reaches up cupping my face with both of his hands as he gently puts his lips on mine. I run my hands across his chest feeling his muscles in his shirt and slide my hands up behind his neck into his hair. He growls and pulls me tighter into him deepening the kiss. He finally releases me and steps back with a smile.

"I got to go." He says as he pushes a few strands of my hair behind my ear. "I may be a little busy this week with the shop, so it may be a few days before I can see you again. But, I will text and call when I can."

"Okay." I say as he kisses my head and heads towards his bike.

After Timber left, I went to take a shower and had just lain down on my bed to watch a little TV before going to bed when I noticed my phone blinking to indicate I had an unread message. When I opened it, there were two messages from that same unknown number.

"You thought you could get away."
"I will have what should have been mine."

I dropped the phone back down on the nightstand and rushed to go check all the doors making sure all the locks were engaged. For a while afterward, I sat huddled on the couch under a blanket. Every sound I heard, causing me to jump nearly out of my skin. Around 3am, I finally drifted off to sleep right there on the couch with all the lights on.

Chapter 5

Timber

The custom bike the guys busted their asses on over the weekend was picked up Tuesday night without a problem. I was proud of my guys putting in so much over time redoing a job that was fucked up by someone looking to set us back. It was now Thursday and all the guys were back from the drop this morning as well. Everyone was looking forward to a long weekend to party and relax.

I had kept in touch with Mina through texts all week. Never in my life had I ever gone out of my way to try to get to know a girl. In our conversations I never let on that I had overheard her side of the conversation she had with her brother Sunday night. I had a lot of unanswered questions about her brothers plus what ever it was that had caused her to be so afraid that she left home. I could tell that she hadn't seen them in a long time and apparently not from them not trying. It was her, she didn't want them around. It was also apparent that she didn't want anyone to know anything about them.

The few times I had talked to her on the phone this week, she had sounded a little off. It could be from doubts about me and I couldn't blame her. This week had been extremely busy with everything that was going on, which is why I called her earlier to let her know we were having a party tonight and I wanted her here. She should be here within the hour so I decided I'd go ahead and take a shower to get the grease off of me from where I was breaking down a motor for a rebuild.

As I walked back into the clubhouse, I could see all the coyotes running around to get everything ready for the party. We rarely had public parties that were open to outsiders, but tonight's was open to anyone. Although most of the town was afraid of us, we'd still have a packed house tonight. They couldn't resist the lure of hanging out with bikers of a 1% club. There was only one rule for them to follow if they wanted in and that was that no cameras or cell phones were allowed inside the door.

I had almost made it down the hall to my door when a soft hand on my shoulder stopped me. I could tell who it was before even turning around. Only one woman here couldn't seem to take no as an answer.

"Hey, Timber, where are you headed off to?" Vivi purred as she moved her hand up to the back of my neck.

"I am going to take a shower to get ready for the party. You are supposed to be helping the other yotes in the kitchen." I say as I pull her hands off of me.

"Do you need any help in the shower? I could wash your back and you could wash mine, while we both get all slick and wet." She replies while rubbing her tits into me.

"I have already told you to knock that shit off. I didn't want you a year ago and nothing about that has fucking changed. My girl will be here tonight and I suggest you behave. I know about you talking to her Sunday night and I am telling you now, if you make trouble between Mina and I, you will fucking regret it!" I say through gritted teeth as I push her away from me and walk through my bedroom door, locking it behind me.

The crazy bitch had better stay away from Mina. I already knew about all the times she had threatened some of the other club girls I had fucked in the past. The rest of them all knew the score but I could tell as soon as I laid eyes on Vivi for the first time that she was the type looking for way more. While all the girls had hopes a brother would put his patch on her back and it had happened in the past, they quickly let those hopes die after being with the club after so many months. It wasn't common for a brother to share his old lady and coyotes were shared by all the brothers.

Checking the clock beside my bed, I quickly went into my bathroom to get my shower. I needed to get Vivi's nasty ass perfume off of me before Mina could get here and smell it on me. I didn't want her to think she was like the rest of them. She wasn't. She was different and I was ready to make her understand that this thing between us was most definitely going to happen.

****

Mina

I had been an absolute nervous wreak all week, jumping at every slight sound my ears could pick up. All kinds of things had started happening. Every morning I found a rose petal on my front door step and the weird text messages hadn't stopped either. I was scared and the only times I had calmed down were the few times I got to hear Timber's voice on the phone. As I was driving to pick up Bella, I kept constant watch to see if I was being followed.

Bella was coming out of the front door of her house as I pulled into the driveway to wait for her. I started laughing as I watched her open the truck door and try to climb into the seat. She gives me the evil eye while reaching to put on her seat belt once she's settled into the seat.

"Where have you been all week? And what's with the dark circles under your eyes" she asks looking over at me.

"I just haven't been sleeping very well." I say as I back the truck up and get back onto the road. I can see she doesn't think I am being completely honest but I am hoping she keeps the questions to herself for tonight. Really don't need Timber asking questions because I wasn't yet sure if I wanted to share any of my past with him yet. We really hadn't known each other very long and I didn't want to lose the connection I felt we had.

I know it was getting time to call Matt and Rafe and tell them what was going on but having grown up in an MC, I understood how it worked. The men in the club would want to put me on a lockdown and try to control everything themselves, leaving me completely in the dark as to what would be going on.

Knowing that someone was coming that close to the house while I was asleep inside just to leave a single rose petal on my porch told me I was dealing with a major psycho. I would ask Bella if I could stay with her for a few days but I was afraid that whoever it was would follow me to her house. I didn't want to involve her.

I knew everything was getting worse and starting to escalate. There was more than just a rose petal at the door this morning. I may have been pretty innocent but I definitely knew what cum looked like. The bastard, whoever he was, sat on my porch jerking off while watching me through the window while I slept.

I would be making that call to my brothers tomorrow. But I was going to take tonight to forget about everything. I wanted just one night before my brothers descended on my house after finding out about my stalker.

We finally pull into the gate at the clubhouse and park towards the back. The music was loud, even out here in the parking lot, indicating that the party was already in full swing. We walk through the door and start trying to make our way through the crowd.

"It's so packed in here, let's head to the bar. We'll be able to see more and hopefully Fang will tell me where to find Timber." I holler loud enough for her to hear me. She just answers with a shake of her head and follows right behind me.

Once at the bar, I can see that all the stools are filled up. Fang notices me and waves me forward.

"Hey, Timber told me to watch for you to come in. Hold on and I will get him up here." He pulls his phone from his pocket and starts typing. A second later, he looks up and says, "He's on his way, doll, shouldn't take long."

As I scan the crowd I see it open up and part as every person makes way for the President of the MC to walk through. His eyes snatch mine and hold steady as he stalks towards me. Watching him come towards me with a possessive look in his eyes has my panties getting wet and I can't help but squeeze my thighs together.

"Hey baby." He says as he leans in to give me a chaste kiss on the lips before leaning away again with a smile. "Come on, me and some of the guys have a table in the back." I take hold of his hand as Bella and I follow him back through the crowd towards the back.

The table that he leads us to is already packed. I was just about to ask about seats when Timber sits and pulls me down into his lap. As I look back up at Bella standing next to the table, Blade reaches over and grabs her by the waist to pull her into his own lap. The look she shoots him causes him to smirk at her and has me wondering if my friend just might kill him tonight.

Timber must have put in a drink order for us already as one of the club girls delivers Bella and me a few shots and a couple beers. I lean down to Timber's ear and say Thank you, kissing his ear before I lean back up. His hand squeezes my thigh in response.

Several hours later, I was seriously buzzed but I could tell that Bella was straight up drunk. She was currently curled up on Blade's lap with one hand at the nap of his neck playing with his hair. Every once in a while he'd look down smiling at her and kiss the top of her head before going back to talking with the other guys.

I was also laid back and comfortable in Timber's lap while he rubbed his thumb along my exposed skin between my top and my pants. My panties had long since completely soaked through. I briefly wondered if he could feel it on his thigh. I was trying very hard not to move too much but the longer he touched me, the harder that was starting to be.

"Having a good time, baby?" He asks with his lips against my ear and it takes everything I have not to moan at the feeling.

"Yes, this has been a pretty good night but I think Bella and I may have had too much to drink to drive back home."

"Don't worry about it. I had no intention of you leaving here tonight." He says as he pulls me even closer.

"What about Bella?"

He looks up from me over to where Bella is snuggled up into Blade and says, "I think Blade has Bella covered. He will take care of her and make sure she is safe."

I look back over at them myself and Blade nods his head at me as he pulls Bella closer to him to whisper in her ear. She jerks back away but he holds her tightly to him before slamming his mouth down on hers. He growls something to her that I can't quite hear but I think he told her to behave. He then pulls her head back down to his chest and goes back to drinking his beer. I definitely need to talk with Bella tomorrow and see what all of that is about.

■■■■■■■■■■■■■■■■■■■■■■■■■■■■■■■■■■■■■■ ■■

Chapter 6

Timber

It was 1am and most everyone had already left to go home. Blade and I had moved to the bar when my girl and Bella seemed to get their 2nd wind around midnight. They were currently dancing along to some older country tunes they had found on the old juke box in the corner.

"I got to ask, brother, about this thing between you and Bella." I say as I turn back towards Blade. I watch him look over towards the girls and shake his head.

"I don't know, man. All I can tell you is that right now she won't allow there to be a something between us." He says.

"But you want there to be?" He nods at me in answer. "Look, you know me; I'm not going to be in the middle of your business. All I am going to say is for you to be absolutely certain and for you not to hurt her. Mina means a lot to me and I want time to see where it can go. I don't want your shit to come between her and me."

He shakes his head as I hear our girls coming back towards us. Right before they get to the bar, we hear a loud explosion. Dane, our newest prospect comes running inside the door as the other brothers that had already went to their rooms earlier come running down the hall.

"Prez, you and the VP need to see this." He says looking back and forth between us.

"Mina, you and Bella stay at the bar. Fang, make sure they stay put." I say as the rest of us walk towards the door.

"Please be careful." Mina says and I look back at her. I expect to see the reactions of a typically woman. The same type of reaction that Bella is currently having, looking truly shaken and scared. But she doesn't have that look. She seems to be completely calm and in control of her emotions.

"I'll be careful. Take care of Bella. We'll be back soon."

We follow Dane around to the back of the parking lot where we see a vehicle that is completely up in flames.

"That's Mina's truck." Blade says as we walk closer. I can see that he is right.

Turning to Dane, I ask, "Did you see what happened?"

"I went to take a piss and not 5 minutes after I get back to the gate, the truck exploded. I didn't see anyone come or go but I can't swear that they didn't." Dane explains.

"Snake!" I yell out and he comes towards me from growing crowd of brothers. "I need you to check the security feed from tonight. That's Mina's truck. I need to find out if this was just random or if she was a target."

"I'll work on it all night if need be and come get you soon as I find anything. Do you think this is connected to the break-in at the shop?"

"I don't know but that is something we need to find out. Mina hasn't acted quite right all week. I thought it might be because our relationship was so new but now I am not sure of anything. Both of the girls will be staying here, at least for tonight. Guess I need to go break it to my girl that her monster truck is now a pile of ash." I look over at Blood and ask, "You got this?"

"Yeah man, we'll get it put out and have a look at it first thing in the morning." He says as I turn to head back inside to break the news to my girl.

****

Mina

After getting Bella to calm down, I got Fang to give her a bottle of water to drink to help sober her up. After that one explosion, there weren't any other noises or gun fire so I knew Timber and the other guys were fine. At least I hoped they were.

Timber and Blade walked back in 30 minutes later. Blade whispered something to Bella, grabbed her hand and led her down the hall.

"Where are they going?"

"He's going to get Bella settled in for the night." He answers and just keeps looking at me.

I could tell he had something to say but seemed to be hesitant about saying it. "What is it? I can tell you want to tell me something. Did anything happen outside?"

"I'm just going to tell it to you straight. It was your truck that exploded. There's nothing left of it."

"Oh my god, what the hell happened?"

"We don't know. I'm having Snake to look over the security feeds and they will also do a thorough check of what is left of your truck first thing in the morning. I have to ask and its important that you are straight with me, is there anything I should know that you haven't told me?"

I immediately bite my lip and say, "No, of course not." while looking down at the ground. I feel bad about lying to him but until I talk to my brothers, I don't feel right telling him about their MC or my past. I may be a girl but even those of us born into the club learn early on that the Club comes first and technically, I still belonged to the Night Howlers MC, Mississippi Chapter.

****

Timber

She was lying to me. It was written all over her face in the way she wouldn't look at me when she answered my question. I figured she wouldn't tell me even though it hurt like hell she wouldn't. But I certainly couldn't blame her. Bella had already warned me that Mina didn't trust very easily.

"Let me go check with the guys and be sure they got the fire out. Stay here and when I get back, we'll get settled for the night." I told her as I headed back outside.

I found Snake headed back towards the door. "Did you guys get it put out?"

"Yeah, I figured we would leave it where it's at for tonight and we can move it into the shop to get a better look at it in the morning."

"That will work. Listen, I need you to see what all else you can find on Mina. Her life before she moved her, her family, all of it."

"I'll do that while I am checking the security video."

"Thanks brother."

As I come back through the door my eyes immediately look to where Mina is sitting and I head her way. I'm half way across the floor to her when I see her face drain of color. So I rush quickly over to her.

"What's wrong baby?" I say as I put my arm around her. She quickly puts her phone away.

"Nothing. It was nothing." Like hell this is nothing.

"Don't lie to me Mina. I can clearly see something is wrong. You look like you have seen a ghost."

"It was nothing Timber, just leave it alone. It's none of your business anyway."

"You really want to play it this way?" I ask on a growl. She just continues to look at me. I grab her by the arm and start walking her towards the rooms in the back. My room is located at the very end of the hall. I quickly unlock the door and pull her inside shutting us in.

"Give me your phone." I demand with my hand out. I expect her to put up more of a fight but she hands it to me with a smirk on her face which pisses me off. The second I try to access the phone, I realize why she was smirking.

"Stop playing games. What's the fucking pass code Mina?" trying my best to hold in the anger that is steadily rising in my throat.

"I'm not giving you shit! We barely know each other and my life isn't any of your fucking business!" my girl is pissed. Yeah, she belongs to me. She may not know it yet, hell probably will fight me on it, but she's still mine all the same. I decided that after our first kiss Friday night. This is why I still planned on getting access to her phone. The look on her face when I walked back into the bar area told me enough to know that she was truly frightened. I took care of what was mine and she was definitely mine.

"Okay baby" I say as I hand her the phone back. She looks at me suspiciously by the way I quickly change tactics. What she doesn't know is I can get Snake to access her phone for me. I didn't need her pass code to get into it when I had a computer genius on payroll.

As she slips the phone back into her pocket, I close in on her. I back her into the door and cage her in with my arms. My cock starts to harden as I press my nose into the curve of her neck. God, she smells so good. I hear her breathing start to change as I continue to smell her neck. I can't resist using my tongue to lick her pulse point. When I feel her heart beat quicken, I nip her with my teeth. She lets out a mewling sound and steps closer to my body to rub her tits into my chest.

"I can't get enough of your smell baby. Do you feel what you do to me?" I ask as I push my jean covered cock into her. "I want you Mina." I say as I let one of my hands slide down her side to the hem of her shirt pushing it up slightly.

The muscles in her stomach start to jump at the first touch of my fingers on her skin. My fingers continue to travel up as I also continue to lick and nip her neck causing her to let out a moan. The sound making my cock harder than it's ever been. My hand finally reaches her bra and I push it up out of the way. As my thumb glides across her nipple, she grabs me by my leather pulling me as close as possible and grinding into my dick.

I take my other hand away from the wall and grab her by the ass, lifting her up into me with one hand. She immediately wraps her legs around my waist and I carry her over to the bed. Once I sit down with her still wrapped around me, I slam my mouth over hers and pull her into me helping her to grind that sweet pussy into my hard length. My other hand is still on her breast pinching her nipple. Every pinch causes her to grind on me harder. I grab hold of her shirt and pull it off of her rolling us over on the bed positioning her under me. She's wearing one of the sexiest red laced bras I've ever seen and wonder if she's wearing panties that match.

"Timber, please" she says in a sexy ass lust filled way, her blue gaze appearing unfocused.

"Use my real name when we are alone." I growl while looking in her eyes. "Hold on baby, I'll give you what you need. I'll always give you what you need." I say as I unbutton her jeans. I stand up so that I can slip them off of her and as they come off, a pair of red lace panties come into view. I stand back taking her all the way in. Her black hair spilled out across my bed while wearing nothing but that red lace set.

"Absolutely beautiful!" I whisper as I lean back down to kiss her soft lips and down her throat. I push her bra out of the way and gently lick her nipple before putting it in my mouth.

"Oh God, Jaxson." she whispers as I suck on her, using my tongue to push her nipple against the roof of my mouth. After a few more sucks and her moving against me trying to get a better angle against the ache I know she is feeling in her pussy, I move down. Kissing and licking down her stomach and around her belly button. When I reach the top of her panties I rub my nose straight down kissing her pussy though her panties. Her hands grab hold of the bed on either side of her.

"Please, please, please" she whispers over and over again.

"What is it baby? Do you need something?" I ask with a chuckle. I continue my slow torture on her body moving to kiss and lick her thighs. She moves one of her hands to her pussy and I grab it. "No baby. That is mine to play with." I tell her as I move her hand back to the bed.

"Stop torturing me Jaxson!" she screams as I continue to play.

I climb back up her body and hold her face close to mine. "Are you a virgin baby?" I ask and she starts to blush trying to turn away from me.

"Don't turn away darlin', I just need to know." I tell her. She finally shakes her head yes. Although I suspected that she was, having her to confirm it made my balls ache. She was untouched and completely mine. I had never cared about that kind of thing before but for some reason I was extremely happy she had never been touched before me. I would be the only man to ever touch her in this way. But I would have to take it slow with her. I was a big guy, bigger than average and I wanted to make sure that when I finally took her completely, her body was more than ready to let me in.

"I won't take your innocence tonight baby but I promise to make you feel good." I stood up and began to take off my clothes with her watching me the whole time. As I dragged my jeans off along with my boxers, my cock sprang free making her eyes widen as she takes in my entire body. "Don't be afraid. I would never hurt you." I say as I stare back into her eyes.

"I'm not afraid of you." She whispers back and I look deeper into her eyes, eyes that are completely filled with lust. I pull her up and unsnap her bra before laying her back down on the bed. I crawl back over her positioning myself between her legs as I grab a fist full of her hair and kiss her sweet mouth while rubbing my cock into her now soaking wet panties.

I break off the kiss but continue to rub my dick into her until she starts panting. My hands wonder down to her panties grabbing them on the side. I give a quick jerk ripping them off and throwing them on the floor. As soon as my cock slides against her hot wet clit without a barrier, I have to take a second to control my own body. I skate my hand down to the apex of her thighs rubbing two fingers along her slick wet pussy lips.

"I feel how much you want me baby. You are soaking wet and its all for me. But do you feel how much I want you Mina? How hard I am? How much I want to lose control and just slam my cock into your virgin pussy?" I say as I slide one finger into her wet opening.

"Ugh, yes. Jaxson, Yes, yes" she says has she tries to push her pussy down on my finger. I slide a second finger in with the first and her head starts to thrash back and forth. I slowly pump my fingers into her curling them up slightly looking for that magic button on the inside. I know I've found it when her thighs start to quiver.

"That's right baby, ride my fingers while I rub that clit with my cock." I can feel her getting closer as her pussy starts to pulse on my fingers and I start to rub my cock faster along her clit, the fingers of my other hand tightening in her hair as we both race to our orgasms. "Come on baby. I want to feel those juices all over this cock, cum all over my hand." I say to her while speeding up. Her pussy tightens up and I know she's there as she starts screaming my name. I finally lose control and cum all over her stomach and clit. Seeing my cum dripping down the slit of her pussy has got to be the sexiest thing I have ever seen in my life.

I roll to the side of her as I slip my fingers out of her pussy and bring them to my lips. She watches me with sleepy eyes as I suck her juices off my fingers. I scoot us both up on the bed and tuck her into my side wrapping my arm around her.

"Go to sleep baby. I'll wake you up in a few hours." I say while closing my own eyes.

After a few minutes her breathing changes and I can tell she's finally asleep. I slip out of the bed and grab my phone sending a text to Snake. After I send that, I reach down and pull her phone from her pants pocket. I step over to the door barely opening it to see Snake standing there already waiting for me. I hand him the phone without a word and shut the door back before gently getting back into bed pulling Mina back into my arms.

Chapter 7

Mina

The sun was shining in my eyes through the window when I woke up. I noticed right away I was in the room alone. Throwing the covers off of me, I sat up on the side of the bed searching the floor for my clothes. I had just finished putting my boots on when there was a knock on the door.

When I opened the door I saw Bella standing there with a smile on her face. "How did you sleep? Blade told me about your truck." She said as she come in and sat down on the bed.

"I slept like a rock." I said with a blush. "I guess I need to call my brothers and let them know. They'll need to call the insurance company."

"I just don't understand what happened. From the way everyone was acting earlier I don't think it was an accident."

"I don't think it was either which is why when I call my brother, I know he's going to come straight here."

"But what's wrong with that Mina? He's your brother and he loves you. I would think that is what most brothers would do."

"You don't understand Bella. I haven't told you everything, the reason why I rarely talk about my life before I left home two years ago or about my brothers."

"Well tell me now. It's not like it's the end of the world. I've always known you've kept a lot to yourself."

"I can't tell, not until I talk with Rafe first. Please? You are my best friend and you deserve to know. I will tell you everything after I talk to him. Promise!"

"Alright, that's good enough for now. Come on; let's go find something to eat."

"Wait a minute. I wanted to ask you about Blade. What's going on with you two?"

"Nothing is going on and nothing is going to go on."

"Why the hell not? I saw how he was acting with you last night. That man is smitten!"

"Smitten or not, the answer is no. He is a part of this club. I am not naïve; I know what goes on around here with those half dressed girls down there in the kitchen. I want no part of it. I will not share my heart with someone that I know can not stay faithful!"

"How exactly do you know he won't stay faithful Bella?"

"Last night proved that I was right. After tucking me into his bed and leaving me there, I got thirsty and decided to try to find the kitchen to get a bottle of water. But when I found the kitchen, he was in there sitting at the table with one of those girls in his lap kissing her."

"Oh, well, I am sorry that happened chica."

"Not as sorry as I am. After pushing him away for weeks, I was really starting to doubt myself. But after seeing that, I am glad I never gave into him." She says with a sad look on her face.

"Well, let's go find that food. I am starving and need to eat before I call my brothers. I'll need all my strength to deal with them."

We leave the room and head towards the kitchen. The coyotes are running around setting out platters of food. I see the girl named Vivi is already sitting down eating and watching the others do all the work. If this was the Night Howlers club house, I would have already dragged her out the door by her hair for not helping the others with the work.

Vivi looks at us as we take a seat at the other end of the table. She looks over at Bella and gives a shit eating grin. Bella just looks down at her plate and starts to eat. I knew right then that it was Vivi in this kitchen last night with Blade. She probably purposely hurt Bella as a way to get to me. I hated the bitch and it was only a matter of time before I kicked her ass.

****

Timber

I had slipped out of bed with Mina early this morning before she woke up so that I could see if Snake was able to find out anything useful.

To say that I was surprised at what he found would be an understatement. She was born into the club life, same as I was. Her father, Axe, had been the President of the Night Howlers for 25 years before losing his life in the same accident as his wife. From the reports, it looked like a brake line had "mysteriously" slipped loose causing him to lose control of the motorcycle. They were both found dead at the scene.

Mina was only 15 at the time, so custody of her was given to her brother, Rafael, who was now the President of the club and known as Reaper. Her brother Matt was also in the same club as Sergeant at Arms and was known as Spark.

She left her home town two years ago and hasn't been back since. There is nothing in here to suggest as to why she left. But I know there has to be a reason. I could tell the other night when she talked to her brother Matt that she really loves and misses them.

"This all you could find, brother?" I ask Snake as I finish reading.

"That's pretty much it. I did find one thing odd though. About a year after her 21st birthday, she enrolled in self defense classes."

"Why would that be odd?"

"It's odd because usually people don't just take those types of classes without a reason. They usually wind up taking them after they have already gone through something. People just don't think about their own safety before that."

"Yeah, I guess you are right. I overheard part of a phone conversation between her and one of her brothers. I could tell from that conversation that something definitely went down. I just don't know what it is and Mina refuses to talk." Soon as I finished talking, Mina's phone started ringing. The display said Rafe and I guessed that to be her other brother. I thought it was a good time to introduce myself.

"Hello?"

"Who the fuck are you?"

"Name is Timber. I assume I have the pleasure of speaking with Reaper?"

"Where the hell is my sister, asshole? If you have hurt her in any way, I will slice your skin off in strips!"

"Just shut the hell up a minute. I haven't hurt Mina. She's sleeping right now and I think you and I need to talk about some shit."

"Why should I talk to you?" he growls through the phone.

"Because someone blew your sisters truck up in the parking lot of my fucking club." I can hear him whispering to someone in the room with him.

"We will be headed out in an hour. Give me an address and a number I can reach you. We can talk then before I take my sister somewhere safe."

"You won't be taking Mina away from here! She is mine! I will be claiming her." I say through clenched teeth.

"We'll see about that when we get there. Text me the address and number, we are headed out your way." He says before hanging up the phone.

I look down at the phone squeezing it in my fist and only letting it go once I hear it starting to crack. If he thinks I will let him take Mina, he has another thing coming. She's fucking mine to protect now. If they wanted to protect her, they should have kept her sexy little ass in Mississippi.

"Trouble?" Snake asks. My temper had gotten to me so badly that I forgot he was still in the room with me.

"Only if he thinks he's taking Mina from me."

"No worries Prez, we won't be letting anyone take your girl. We've all seen you with her. She makes all your hard edges a little softer." He says while laughing.

"What the fuck ever, did you find anything on the surveillance footage from last night?"

"Yeah and from what I can tell it's the same guy. I also found some texts on her phone from an unknown number. It appears to be a burner phone. I wasn't able to trace it. The texts are really crazy and seem to have gotten more frequent the last 2 weeks."

"What did they say?"

"Whoever this person is, they are truly sick in the head. At first they just said things like, *You belong to me; You tried to get away,* etc. The most recent one was sent last night after the truck explosion. It said; *Whore's deserve to burn.* After reading that, I went back and compared the time on the first video from the shop. The break-in happened after you had been sitting with Mina most of the night at Blackcat. You may be able to get some more answers from Mina. Find out if she has any clue who this guy is."

I couldn't believe she had been keeping the text messages a secret. Even if she wasn't ready to let me completely in, why didn't she tell Bella? I know Bella would have told me, at least about this.

"I'll go see what I can get her to tell me. You should get something to eat and crash for a while. You've been up all night. I appreciate you finding what you could."

"That's what I'm here for."

As soon as I open the door to go see if Mina is still in the room asleep, we hear a lot of screaming, cussing, glass breaking and some of the brothers laughing coming from the direction of the kitchen. Snake and I immediately head in that direction.

When I walk through the door, I see that Mina has a screeching Vivi by her hair, pushing her face down into the table top. Vivi is bleeding from the nose but a quick glance at Mina shows me that she is fine.

"What the fuck is going on in here?" I ask causing the entire room to go silent.

****

Mina

The silence around me is deafening as I look up at Timber standing just inside the room. I didn't mean to cause a scene but the bitch had it coming. While we ate, she kept talking to the other coyotes about her time with Blade last night. She only did it to taunt poor Bella. I tried to ignore it like Bella asked me to do but when the bitch tripped her trying to make it look like an accident, all bets were off.

"She was just taking care of a little problem." Blood says with a wide grin before turning to Bella. "How about we go for a walk outside, sweetness?" He asks her, grabbing her hand at the same time Blade comes into the room behind Timber.

"She's not going any where with you." Blade says through clenched teeth.

Timber looks around between all of us and with a sigh he says, "Blood, take Bella for that walk." Which causes Blade to growl but Timber just ignores him. "Mina, let her up off the table and come with me." I immediately let her ass drop to the floor and step over her following Timber back towards his room. Once we are inside, I take a seat on his bed and just wait.

"Mind telling me what the hell happened out there?"

"Bella walked in on Blade and Vivi in the kitchen last night. Vivi must have seen her before she ran back to her room. We were trying to eat but Vivi kept taunting Bella. She kept talking about her sexual encounter with Blade. I could tell it was making Bella uncomfortable but she asked me to ignore the stupid bitch. Which I honestly tried to do! But when Bella got up to help the girls clear away the dishes, she tripped Bella and tried to act like it was an accident. So I slammed her coyote ugly face into the table."

I can see him trying not to laugh, his lips keep twitching so I just sit there and smile at him. He shakes his head and then walks over to me, tilting my face up to him.

"You are really something else." He says before he kisses me, and God, what a kiss. I don't think I will ever get enough of this mans kisses. He pulls away much too soon in my opinion.

"We need to talk about some things I found out this morning." He says looking extremely serious.

"Like what?" I reply as he pulls something out of his back pocket. One look tells me it's my phone. "Why do you have my phone?" My heart rate starts to pick up at the thought of what he could have found on it.

"I wouldn't have taken your phone if you had just been honest with me last night when I asked if there was anything I needed to know. Since I could tell you were hiding shit, I took the phone and let Snake have a look." He says to me with a raise brow.

I can tell from that look that he probably now knows almost everything. I knew how this all works, I grew up in it. There was always someone in the club or an outside connection that could get information that most people couldn't get a hold of.

"So I guess you now know everything." I state.

"I know most of it but I know there are some pieces I have yet to get and you are going to tell me everything."

"I need to talk to my brother before I tell you anything." I'm starting to get pissed off that he thinks he can take control like this. It's a reminder of why I left home to begin with. The men in my life always thinking they can control everything and dictate to me how to live my own life.

"Ah, yes, you mean your brother Reaper? No worries, he's on his way here."

"What the hell do you mean he's on his way here?"

"He called while I had your phone and yes, I answered it. They should be here by lunch time tomorrow."

"You had no right to neither go through my phone nor answer it Timber!" I scream at him.

He grabs me by my arms getting close to my face while he shakes me a little bit. "I had every right! Whether you want to agree with me right now or not, you are MINE! The second I touched you for the first time, I knew it. And I know that you felt that shit too. You are mine and I protect what belongs to me!" He growls just before slamming his mouth down on my own.

At first I stand as stiff as possible but there is no way for me to fight it. My body betrays me because it already knows that it belongs to him. I finally relax into his kiss which causes him to soften against me as well. He slowly backs out of the kiss, cupping my face in his calloused palm.

"You can't tell me that you didn't feel that. Your body responds the second I get close to you." He whispers against my lips before backing away.

I stare at him for a moment and ask, "What do you want to know?"

"First I want you to tell me about these text messages you have been getting. Is that the only thing that has been happening?"

"No." I sigh before turning and sitting down on the bed. "I started noticing a single rose petal being left on my front porch about a month ago. I didn't think anything of it until I received the first text message. And then yesterday morning I saw what I am sure was cum along with the rose petal."

"What the fuck! Mina, are you serious right now? Someone has been stalking you and coming to your house while you are there and you don't say a fucking word to anyone?"

"I was planning on calling my brother today to tell him what was going on. Then I was going to find a hotel to stay at for a bit. I just wanted one night without them coming in and taking over my life again! Besides, I can take care of myself. I'm no longer that scared, frightened girl from four years ago."

"I'm sure those self defense classes taught you a few tricks." He says making me gasp. "Yeah, Snake found that tidbit of information as well. What I want to know is what the hell happened to you that caused you to take a self defense class for a year before taking off from home and never going back?"

I knew that eventually I would have to talk about my past. It really wasn't as bad as it could have been. Some women aren't able to escape before getting raped. I happened to be lucky that I did get away.

"Come on Mina, just be honest with me. Tell me what happened. I'd rather find out from you than from your cocky ass brother when he gets here."

"Fine, I'll tell you." I sigh. "There was a guy in my brothers club. He was a little older than me but he made it clear that he was interested. He was kind, sweet and very attentive. I was used to all the guys being nice to me. They all treated me like a sister except for him. Mostly because I grew up with all the other guys and Josh was a new guy to the club. We had been dating for about 2 months when my 21st birthday came around."

"I had been learning to drive an old bike Rafe had in the garage. For my birthday, my brothers surprised me with a brand new Harley Davidson Sportster. It was beautiful! I went for a ride and stayed gone all day, only coming back in time for the pool party later that afternoon. I had just pulled my new bike into the shed when Josh came in from a side door. I could tell he'd already been drinking. I don't remember everything that was said but I remember thinking I needed to get out of there.

He grabbed me and hit me in the face causing me to fall on the ground. When he got on top of me, I started to struggle and he hit me several more times in the face. He just about had my pants and panties off of me when Grease came in. He seen what was happening and got him off." With tears in my eyes I look up at Timber. "That's everything, happy now?"

He sits down on the bed pulling me into his lap and holds me close allowing me to cry into his shoulder.

"Shhh, baby, its okay, I got you now."

"He'd never acted out of the way to me before. I felt so afraid." I tell him.

"Is that why you finally left and never went back home or allowed your brothers back into your life?"

"Yeah, I guess. Every night when I'd try to sleep, I'd have nightmares about it and all I could see was that damn leather cutt of his. He broke me. I couldn't stand to be around the other guys simply because of the cutt they were wearing. It didn't matter that I grew up with most of them and knew they would never hurt me like he did. After a year of sleepless nights, I signed up for the defense class. But that didn't get rid of the nightmares. So I left. I needed time away to get my head back straight so I could be around my family again without them having to tiptoe around me as if they were afraid I'd shatter like glass."

"There's no reason to hold your family back any more Baby. You got the time you needed away from the club and you are no longer broken. If you were, you'd have never let me get close to you. But since you did, I'm not ever letting you go Mina. Do you understand? I know we've not been together that long and we are still getting to know each other but I want to see where this thing between us will go. I need to know if you want that too."

I can see the sincerity in his eyes as he speaks, the words flowing straight to my heart. I know in that moment that I could fall in love with this man. I'm probably already halfway there but these feelings frighten me.

"I'm not sure if I can promise you anything Timber. Every thing feels right when I am with you but it's been a long time since I put myself out there. And as you know, last time I did it turned into a disaster that took me years to get past."

"Just give me a chance, Mina. Not everyone in this life will break your trust in them."

He reaches over to tuck a strand of hair behind my ear as he leans in for a kiss. The second his tongue touches my bottom lip, I open my mouth to him. Goosebumps spread all over my body causing my nipples to become hard and tingly. He deepens the kiss even more while I rub my aching tits into his chest. He lets out a growl and pushes me down onto the bed with him on top of me.

"Can you feel that?" He asks while rubbing his hardness into me. "I am like this all the time Mina. All I have to do is think of you. The color of your hair, the way your eyes look at me. It all lights up my body like a fire I can't extinguish."

His words along with his movements are turning me on so bad that I am panting for breath. There's a pressure building inside of me and I keep trying to rub my pussy into him harder.

"Timber..."

"What's my name baby?" He growls as he lifts both my arms above my head and holds them with one of his own.

"Jaxson?" I say looking into his eyes while trying to focus through the fog of lust.

"Yes, that is the name I want to always hear while we are alone." His free hand slides my shirt up my ribs barely touching the underside of my breast but he doesn't go any farther before his hand starts on a downward path to my jeans. He unsnaps them and pulls the zipper down, sliding his hand inside. The second his finger touches my clit, I feel like my body is on fire.

"You may not be ready to tell me that you belong to me but your body does not lie. One touch and you are soaked for me. I want nothing more than to fill your pussy up with my cock and pound into you until I fill you up with my cum. Afterwards, I will do it all again until I know you are so full of me every other man can smell it."

"Oh, God." I say as he rubs my clit even faster. I'm just on the cliff of my orgasm but before I can fall over it, he removes his hand. "What? Don't stop Jaxson. I was so close!"

"Until you tell me that you are mine and that you are willing to give us a chance, I plan to keep you in a constant state of arousal so that you understand how you make me feel all the time. But the minute you say you are mine, Mina, I plan to bring you to this room and make you scream my name so many times you lose your voice." He moves off the bed and looks down at me with a smirk on his face before leaving the room.

Chapter 8

Timber

Snake was crossing our parking lot towards me. "Hey Prez! There's a cop at the front gate asking to talk to you!" He said as he walked up to me. "I told him I didn't know if you were here and I wasn't letting him in without a warrant. He wouldn't tell me what it was about."

"Has anyone in the crew done anything I should know about? We don't need any more problems right now."

"Far as I know, everyone has been staying out of trouble."

"Let's hope that is the case. Go ahead and let the cop in. I either talk to him now or we risk him coming back later. I'll be at a table in the bar." I say as I walk back towards the clubhouse.

Walking back into the bar, I spotted Bear. "There's a cop headed in. Go tell everyone to keep a low profile while he's here." I told him.

"On it." He said as he walked out the back door. Fang, one of our prospects was manning the bar. I gave him a chin lift and knew he'd bring me a beer. As I sat down the door opened and a tall man in a brown sheriff uniform walked in behind Snake and Blade. I figure him to be in

his mid-fifties and definitely a proud man with
the way he carries himself. I motioned for him to
take a seat.

"John Wilson." He says offering me his hand.

"Timber. Now, what can I help you with?" I
say while shaking his hand and Fang sets a beer
down in front of me.

"There's been some activity south of here.
Four young women are missing and the only
leads we have is a neighbor that says she
heard motorcycles."

"What does that have to do with my
club? Are you accusing us of something,
sheriff?" I say with anger in my voice as
Blade and Snake tense up next to the table.

He immediately throws his hands up shaking
his head back and forth. "No, not at all, I meant
no disrespect to you. Please, I came here for
your help. We've been researching your club for
a long while now. We know that when you took
over the club from your father seven years ago
the dynamics of The Wolfsbane MC started to
change. All of you have worked hard to turn this
club around by opening up more legal
businesses and keeping your noses clean. It's
why you are no longer on the FBI's radar nor on
ours. And we also know that even in your less

savory dealings your club never hurt women or children."

He sits back waiting for what he just said to sink in with us. I give him a chin lift for him to continue.

"One of the young women missing is my niece, Miranda Grayson." He says as he lays a picture on the table between us. I pick it up and see a pretty red head that looks to be in her early 20s. I hand the picture to Snake as the sheriff continues.

"We know the night she disappeared from her house; she got off work around midnight and stopped at a gas station about 3 miles from her house around 15 minutes after leaving work. We confirmed that with surveillance from the store. Her neighbor reported something being wrong at the house at around 9am the following morning. The side entrance door was broken. So we know that has to be the point of entrance. There appears to have been a struggle in the bedroom and there was a partial blooded finger print on the wall. There wasn't a lot of blood, just a few drops leading out the same broken door. The blood sample came back to show that it was Miranda's." He says while appearing to struggle not to show emotion.

"What is it you need from us exactly?" I ask.

"As I said, I know that your club appears to be totally legal these days. But I also know you still have plenty of contacts with the clubs that are on the other side of the law. I want your help to find these girls. My niece is all I have left of my sister and I swore I would protect her."

"Do you have any leads other than just a witness that heard motorcycles?"

"There have been reports of one particular club not from the area that has been causing minor issues. They aren't even from this state."

"Who?" I ask.

"The Demon Riders."

I sit back studying this man in front of me. He must truly be desperate if he was coming to us for help. He was right; we never hurt women or children. We believed it took a true monster to do something like that. Your soul could never come back from hurting an innocent.

"I'll have to take this to the entire club before I can promise anything. But if we do this, you have to share with us everything you know. All police files, evidence, everything you have or will get."

"I understand and agree to those terms." He says finally looking a little relieved since walking in here.

"I'll be in touch soon as I meet with the rest of my club." I watch him walk back out the door and I turn to Blade, "Call all the guys in for church. Tell them to be here at 7." I say as I check the time and head towards the shop to check in on the orders we have going out this next week.

An hour later I am in the kitchen grabbing a bottle of water when I hear someone come in behind me and clear their throat.

"Hey Bella, did you need something?"

"I was going to ask if you can get me a ride home. There's paperwork that needs to be finished over at the coffee shop. I also need to get my orders in over the phone or I won't have enough supplies to last next week."

"I'll get Blade to run you home." I say as I grab my phone to text him.

"Can you get someone besides Blade?" She asks while looking down at the ground. I walk over to her and put my hand on her shoulder and give it a squeeze.

"I'm not exactly sure what went on in this kitchen last night but I would bet it wasn't what you think. Nor was it whatever the hell Vivi was spewing in here early this morning. Blade wouldn't willingly hurt those he cares about."

"Thanks for saying that Timber but he is welcome to sleep with anyone he wants. There's nothing between him and I for him to even remotely care about what I think."

"Do you really believe the bullshit that comes out of your mouth Bella?" Blade says through clinched teeth at the door. Neither of us had heard him come into the room. She opens her mouth as if she is about to say something but he cuts her off.

"Just get your ass outside on my bike and I'll take you home." He says as he storms back the way he came.

She looks back at me for just a moment before following in the same direction. I don't know what exactly is going on with those two but hopefully they will get it worked out.

****

Mina

After Timber left me a panting frustrated mess on the bed, I laid there for about thirty minutes wishing I had clean clothes so I could shower before getting up and fixing my clothes back. Dane, another prospect for the club, knocked on the door and handed me a duffle bag explaining that Timber had arranged for some of my clothes to be brought to the clubhouse. He'd also made sure that my laptop was brought as well. After getting cleaned up in the shower I sat on the bed working on my book.

I got so lost in my story again that I didn't realize how long I had been working until a noise at the door caused me to raise my head. Timber was standing there leaning against the door watching me with a smile.

"How long have you been standing there?"

"A good 15 minutes or so." He chuckles. "What are you writing? It must be really good to draw your attention so completely."

"It's not anything you would want to read."

"What makes you think I wouldn't read it?"

"It's a romance novel and men like you do not read romance novels." I explain to him.

"Mina, if you wrote it, I am going to read it."

I immediately start blushing at the thought of him reading my book, especially the sex scenes. What would he think of them or of me? I may be limited in my actual experience with sex but I definitely have fantasies. I look back up at him and immediately wonder what it would be like to have this man to tie my hands to the bed while he spanks me. I can feel my face heat up even more and know that I am probably as red as a tomato and I watch his smile grow even bigger.

"Just what is going through that pretty little head of yours?" he asks.

I clear my throat, "Nothing. Did you need something?"

"There're several things I need right now baby." He growls. "But I thought you may be hungry. The girls said they hadn't seen you all afternoon. So take a break and come eat with the rest of us."

I close down my computer and walk over to him, taking his hand. He pulls me in close and kisses my neck.

"Mmm, yeah, definitely smells like dessert. I'll need another taste soon to be sure though." He whispers across my skin. I gasp as I feel the immediate reaction of my body to his words. He leans back to see my face and just sends that sexy smile at me before taking my hand again and walking towards the kitchen.

After we finish eating, Timber tells me he called everyone in tonight for church at 7 and would come find me after they finished up. I set about to help the girls get the kitchen cleaned up before I head back to the bedroom.

For a little while I try to get some more work done but my mind keeps going back to what Timber said about what he'd do to me when I finally gave in to telling him I was his. It turned me on just thinking about it. My phone starts ringing, interrupting my thoughts and I answer it without looking at the display.

"Hello?"

"Have you missed me little Fairy?"

"Who is this?" I ask with a shaky voice although I am afraid that I already know.

"I know it's been four years but surely you haven't forgotten the first man to ever put his finger in that tight little pussy" He says as I start to shake all over and flashes of memory swirl in my head.

"Josh, what the fuck do you want?"

"I'm coming for what should have been mine. Your little boyfriend and his club can't stop me. I ride with a new crew now and we will destroy his pussy ass club."

"My brothers will kill you this time."

"Your brothers have been chasing me since you left home sweet little Mina and they haven't found me yet. No one will save you this time. You won't even see me coming. I really can't wait to shove my cock up your ass while you scream. See you soon, *Little Fairy.*" He growls through the phone before hanging up.

After four years, I had started to think that I was finally safe and it took only one phone call to destroy that illusion. Hearing his voice again after so long had me just as scared as I was the night he attacked me.

I told Timber everything I could remember from that night but I didn't tell him that I couldn't remember all of it. I had blacked out after he hit me so many times in the face. What other few details I knew about was from what the Doctor had found during her examination of me at the clubhouse.

Deciding that I should go wait for Timber to finish up church so that I can tell him about the phone call, I head towards the bar area to get a drink.

****

Timber

We all get settled around the table in the meeting room and I wait for my men to settle down before I start.

"I had an impromptu meeting with Sheriff Wilson earlier today. He showed up when I was headed out. Apparently, he needs our help."

"What the hell could the cops need our help with?" asks Butcher, our Road Captain.

"He says that some activity has been going on a little south of us. And apparently 4 young women have come up missing from their homes. One of which is his niece, Miranda Grayson. They don't have a lot of evidence to go on. He said he has looked into the background of our club and seems to think he can trust us enough to help locate and find the missing girls. I said I would bring it to the entire club for a vote. We all will need to agree before I lend him our help. I know it's not like us to help or side with the cops but we are talking about innocent young women. And we may be the best help they have of surviving, if they are even still alive."

"Who do they think did it? They must have some thoughts on who they think it was." Bear asks.

"They are leaning towards it being the Demon Riders. They have been spotted in the areas, causing problems."

"If we do this, he needs to be forthcoming with all information they have at the station. We don't need to be kept in the dark on anything that may get ourselves killed." says Blood, our sergeant at arms. I look over at Snake who seems deep in thought.

"Snake, you want to share your thoughts?"

"Remember what I told you earlier about the partial tattoo I was able to see on the video? I am wondering if this guy is somehow connected to whoever took these girls. The Demon Riders have been connected to prostitution rings for years." he says.

"Do you think you can hack into their computer systems and maybe try to track where they are? If we can find out for sure if they are in the area, it would give us a better idea of where to start looking. Since we already suspect this guy in the video of having something to do with what is going on with Mina, I will be assigning one of you to be with her whenever I can't be."

"I'll get started right now." He says as he grabs his laptop.

"So, I need to know what you all think. If this is something all of you are willing to do. To align ourselves with the law and help find these girls." Ask them all while looking at each man. "Let's put it to a vote. It has to be unanimous. All in favor?" I ask and every man at the table says "Aye".

"Okay. Snake you continue to see what you can find. Let us know soon as you do. Blade, contact the sheriff and let him know we are in.

Tell him we need a copy of all his files. Soon as you have them, give them to Snake. Butcher, you and Blood, start calling our contacts and see if anyone has seen a Demon Rider in their area. Also, just so everyone knows, Mina's brothers are coming in from Mississippi. They should be here by lunch time tomorrow. Her oldest brother is the President of the Night Howlers."

"Holy shit, are you serious?" Blood asks. "They control the majority of the Southern coast!"

"That would be them. Reaper is not very happy that his sister is here and plans to try to take her somewhere safe. I won't let that happen. She stays with me. I plan on making her my ole lady. Her brother is under the impression she still belongs to the Night Howlers but the way I see it, he let her leave two years ago which severed that tie. I'm now claiming her as property of Wolfsbane. Are there any objections?"

"Hell no, there won't be any objections at this table, Prez. We are all happy for you." Snake says while everyone shakes their head in agreement with him.

"Then if there is nothing else, church is dismissed."

We all file out and head towards the bar. I spot Mina as soon as I walk in and head her way. When I slip my arms around her from behind she jumps a little bit before relaxing against me.

"Why are you so jumpy baby?"

"He called me Timber." Her admission causes all my muscles to tense up. Her eyes are full of fear. She didn't even look like this when she told me about the rose petals and cum on her porch.

I try to get control over my anger, there's no way that I want her to think it's directed at her.

"What did he say? I need to know everything he said."

She picks up the shot glass that is sitting in front of her and downs it. After Dane, who is manning the bar tonight, refills her glass, she downs it quickly as well.

"Come on baby, slow down on the shots. Just tell me what he said."

"He said he was coming for me and that you wouldn't be able to stop him. He said he would destroy your entire club and that he rode with a new crew these days that couldn't be stopped." A lone tear escapes from her eye and I lean in grabbing her face wiping it away with my thumb.

"He's not going to hurt you. You are mine and I will kill him if he ever touches you again." I say as I pull her in for a hug.

"Come on baby, you need some rest. Your brothers will be here tomorrow."

"Oh, God, don't remind me." She groans causing me to chuckle as I lead her back to my room.

Once we are in our room, I shut and lock the door before turning to look at her. She is so beautiful. I don't know how she got under my skin. It started the very first time I laid eyes on her when she walked into *Blackcat* with Bella. I know she is it for me but I only have until tomorrow to convince her. I'm afraid that she will choose to go with her brothers tomorrow instead of staying here with me.

I reach back and pull my shirt off over my head and toss it in the floor as I walk towards her. Her eyes are on me and I see lust fill her eyes as she glances across my chest and arms.

When I am finally standing right in front of her, I slowly grab the hem of her shirt and lift it over her head revealing her firm breasts in a black bra. My cock starts to swell and throb in my jeans.

"Take the rest off baby and get in the bed." I rasp, trying to keep control of myself.

Instead of doing what I said, she reaches out with her hand and outlines the wolf tattoo that is on my chest. Having her hands touch me so softly makes me let out a groan.

"Mina, you need to do what I said before I lose control. I don't want to take you until you admit that you are mine."

"I want you to make me yours Jaxson." I look into her eyes and see lust. But I also see fear there which makes me think she's just afraid she may not have this chance again.

"I can see the fear in your eyes baby. Nothing is going to happen to you. I won't let it so there's no reason to give in just because you think things are going to go wrong."

"I don't think that is the kind of fear that I am feeling." She admits with a blush and I begin to smirk.

I stick my hands into her hair and grab the back of her neck pulling her closer to me.

"Are you afraid of my cock Mina?"

"I think I am more afraid of how you make me feel." She whispers up to me.

Slamming my mouth down on hers I immediately feel the magic that is always there every time I touch her. She's like a witch that has cast a spell on me or maybe she's a fairy that sprinkled pixie dust on my cock.

I walk her backwards towards the bed. When the back of her knees hit the side, I break off the kiss and lay her back as I pull her pants off taking her panties at the same time. I stand back and take off the rest of my clothes as she unhooks her bra and tosses it to the floor with everything else.

I step back to the bed and skim my hands up her thighs making them quiver. Pushing her legs open with my shoulders, I get a full view of the prettiest pussy.

"I can see how wet your pussy already is for me." I tell her. She immediately tries to close her legs but I don't budge.

"Don't move baby, I'm finally going to get my dessert." I growl just before I lick her folds getting a taste of her essence.

I rub the tip of my tongue into her clit rapidly as I ease a finger into her curling it up to find her g-spot. I know I have found it when she grabs my hand to hold me in place as if she's afraid I'll stop.

When she starts pushing her pelvis toward me, sucking my finger deeper into her pussy, I suck her clit into my mouth and suck hard. She comes in a gush all over my hand and quickly I replace my finger with my tongue until she is left with nothing but after shocks.

I move up over her, rubbing my cock along her folds, covering it in her juices.

I look into her eyes and say, "Are you sure? Once you give yourself to me, you are mine. You become part of Wolfsbane but more importantly, you become my ole lady. You will wear my patch and one day soon you'll wear my ring."

"I'm sure Jaxson. I've never been more sure of anything else."

I grab her by the neck and kiss her thoroughly.

"I plan to take you bare. There will never be anything between you and me when we are in our bed together. If you don't want kids right now, I would suggest making an appointment with the doctor to get on the pill."

She looks at me with wide eyes like she can't believe what I just said.

"You talk like you don't care if I get pregnant Jaxson."

"That's because I don't care. I think it would be nice to have some little girls running around that look like you. They would be ours. Now hush and let me love you."

I kiss down the side of her neck as my hands tweak her nipples. She gasps and rubs her pussy into my cock a little harder. I suck one of her nipples into my mouth and bite down just a little bit. Her tits are so sensitive, I notice that every time I bite them a little bit, her pussy gushes and gets wetter. I start rubbing my cock into her faster and when I know she is close to another orgasm I position the head directly at her center easing just the head in.

My thumb begins circling her clit as I slowly push more of my cock into her tight little hole.

"That pussy is so tight baby. It feels so good on my cock. Let me all the way in." I say as I ease a little farther into her.

I flick my thumb even faster on her clit making her move on her on and her pussy takes even more of me. I pull almost completely out, leaving only the head in her entrance when she wraps her legs around me and jerks me all the way into her.

Feeling her tense up once I am fully inside, I look into her eyes and kiss her.

"I was trying to go slow so I wouldn't hurt you." I say against her lips.

"I knew it would hurt the first time Jaxson, but you were going too slow. I need you to move." She says as she attempts to move up and down on my shaft.

"Is this what you want baby." I say as I ease out and slowly move back in.

"Oh yes, like that. Just don't stop."

I start a slow rhythm as I alternate between biting and licking each of her nipples. They are a direct line to her pussy making her passage even slicker with her juices.

"Harder." She whispers.

I grab two fists full of her hair and growl as I begin to slam into her harder than before. I rise up on my knees, tilting her up and slamming back into her at this new angle causing her to gasp.

"Play with those beautiful tits while I pound this pussy baby."

I watch as she begins to tweak her own nipples and her pussy pulses every time she pinches them. My strokes become even harder as I fuck her.

"Come on baby, cum on my cock. Let those juices drip down my balls." I growl at her.

I feel her pussy start to tighten fiercely around me. Looking down, I watch as her pussy swallows up my entire cock and the second she screams out my name in the middle of her orgasm, I let the fire in my balls go and fill her womb with my seed.

Chapter 9

Mina

The next morning, I woke up to Timber slowly kissing me. I didn't remember falling asleep but I do remember him waking me up several times throughout the night to make love to me again. He awoke something in me and made me feel like I was extremely special. I had never felt like this with anyone else which is why I had never let any other relationships get far enough to take the next step.

"Come on baby. We need to get us some breakfast. I'm pretty sure I used up all your energy last night." He says with that cocky smile on his beautiful face before pulling on clean clothes. "Plus, your brothers should be getting here soon. I'm sure you'd like to greet them in the bar instead of our bedroom."

"Well, I really would hate to see them kill you within the first five minutes of meeting you." I get up and start pulling clothes out of my bag. Once we are dressed, we head to the kitchen.

After breakfast, Timber heads over to the hop to get some work done before lunch and I stay to help the yotes clean up. Vivi sits at the table the whole time glaring at me and not helping. I think it's time I put some fire under her ass and let it be known that I will not be pushed around by the club pussy. I know that being the President's Ole Lady requires that I take control in this area.

"Vivi, I would suggest you get up and start helping to get shit cleaned up in this kitchen. After that, you can help with the clothes that are piling up in the laundry room."

"Who the hell do you think you are to tell me what to do? Do you really think that just because you are fucking the President you are special? HA! You are no different than the rest of us!" She screeches at me.

"I am going to tell you one last time to get your ass up and help the other girls around here, or I will throw you out of this building and into the street beyond the gates! We can do this the easy way or the hard way. You choose." I say, having enough of her shit.

"You can't do that! Timber will not let you, you stupid bitch! You're not in charge here! You are only doing this because you know he'll be fucking my pussy when he's done with you next week!"

"Vivi, you are so damn delusional! A club brother is not going to take a filthy whore like you to be his ole lady, especially the President of the club. I also know for a fact Timber has never touched your ass. Do you really think he is going to want a stretched out pussy that probably smells and tastes like tuna? Bless your little heart!" I say with a curl to my lip as the other girls start to laugh.

"Fuck you, bitch!" She screams.

"Guess it's the hard way then." I say just before I grab her by the hair and start for the front door dragging her behind me. She claws at my arm, drawing blood but I hardly notice. Nothing is going to stop me from taking the trash out.

****

Timber

Blood and a few of the other brothers were still going over Mina's truck when I got to the shop after breakfast. They were mainly still trying to find what pieces they could of the bomb that was used.

I went to the office to work on some of the paperwork for our legitimate side of the shop. We had several vehicles scheduled to come in for basic repairs and maintenance. About 45 minutes later I heard a large rumble and knew a lot of bikes were headed in. Guess I was finally going to come face to face with the legendary Night Howlers.

Standing outside the shop, I waited for them all to pull up where Blood directed them to. I spotted Reaper right off in the front leading his crew and walked over to meet him at his bike.

"Reaper." I said as he cut off his engine and climbed off his bike.

"You must be Timber. Where's my sister?" He asks just as we hear a commotion at the front of the clubhouse building. One look tells me Vivi has been up to shit again because I see that Mina is dragging her out by the hair. All the members that were inside and the coyotes too are following behind her.

Reaper starts to chuckle along with his crew as they look on the scene in front of us.

"Never mind, guess we found her. The bitch she's pulling behind her, is that your side piece?" He says as his eyes turn to slits looking at me.

"Hell no, the bitch wishes in her dreams." I growl back at him. "She's been giving Mina and her friend, Bella, problems this past week. Looks like Mina is over playing nice."

"My sister has a temper from hell in case you haven't figured it out yet."

"I probably better go see what the problem is." I say on a sigh as I head in Mina's direction with the Reaper following me.

We catch up with Mina nearly at the front gate and it takes her a second to realize we are standing there. She doesn't let go of the screaming banshee she has a hold of but she stops walking.

"What's going on Mina?" I ask calmly.

"Well, I told this bitch to get up and help the other girls clean up around the clubhouse. She refused. I told her if she didn't help, I would remove her and toss her out the gate. And that is exactly what I plan on doing! Do you plan to stop me?" She says with a stubborn look on her face like she isn't sure what my reaction will be.

"I have no intensions of stopping you. You have all the say in that department baby."

"But Timber, I've been with the club longer than she has!" Vivi says in her whining voice and I look over at her.

"That may be true, but Mina is my girl. That makes her queen bee around here." As I finish saying this, Mina drags her the rest of the way to the gate and pushes her out, slamming the gate back shut.

Vivi continues to scream and threaten Mina saying she'll regret this but I don't worry about that bitch. I won't let anyone hurt my girl. When she walks back towards us, she doesn't go straight to her brother which makes hope flare in my chest that she is definitely accepting her role in my life. I give her a quick kiss on the lips before we look back at her brother and the rest of his crew.

"What? No hug for us Little Fairy?" Reaper asks and Mina moves to give him a hug.

"I missed you Rafe. Where's Matt?" she asks.

"You need to go back to calling us by our club name Little Fairy." He says with a chuckle. "Spark will be here later. He's checking on some club business, shouldn't be more than an hour."

"Why don't you and your crew come inside the clubhouse? I'm sure you all could use a drink after your long ride. Once your other brother gets here, I'll call church and we can all go over everything." I say and we all start walking towards the door.

Once inside, I make introductions to some of my own crew and we take a seat the table in the back. Once I sit down, Mina sits down in my lap without me telling her to. She seems to be trying to make a statement to her brother without saying a word. He seems to understand it clearly as his eyes narrow at us but he doesn't say a word.

I wrap my arms around her and sit back to listen as Mina and her family catch up with each other since she's been gone from home.

****

Mina

"What you been up to Fairy? We haven't seen you in a really long time. We've missed you." Grease asks me as a way to break the tension between me and my brother.

"I've been really good Grease. My editor helped to get me a three book signing deal last year. I'm currently working on the 2nd one."

"That's really awesome. Why didn't you tell Spark and I about that during one of our calls?" Rafe asks with a disappointed tone.

"I don't know. We didn't exactly talk very much the last two years. When we did, it was to argue over you paying my mortgage off." I snap at him. There's no way I am taking all the blame for the tense relationship we have had the past couple of years.

The front door of the clubhouse opens and I see that Matt is walking through the door. I jump up and tart running towards him and he picks me up as I jump into his arms.

"God, I've missed you Matt!!" I say as he puts me back down.

"Ha-ha, yeah I can tell Little Fairy. Look at you! You have grown even more since we seen you last!"

"I was already grown when I left unless you are saying I've gotten fat?" I ask with a serious look on my face trying to not crack up as he tries to answer.

"That's not what I meant. You are still as little as a fairy."

"I'm just messing with you. Come on, Rafe is already at a table with Timber. I want you to meet him." I say with a blush.

Matt grabs my arm to stop me, "Hang on there Fairy. What's that look? Have you finally found what you've been looking for?"

"Yes, I do believe that I have Matt. And I need your help to convince Rafe. He has that stubborn look on his face. I will not let him come here and take over my life. I have no intension of allowing him to take me away from Timber."

He studies my face for a few seconds before shaking his head. "Okay, let's go meet your man and try to keep our brother from killing him before I can get some little nieces or nephews that I can spoil rotten." He says shocking me and reminding me of the conversation Timber and I had last night. He starts laughing when my face turns blood red.

"Just come on." I say in a huff as we walk back to the table in the back.

****

Timber

After being introduced to Mina's brother Matt also known as Spark and the Sergeant at Arms or the Night Howlers, I knew that he was completely on our side. It was just Reaper that I needed to deal with when it came to making sure he didn't try to take Mina from me.

"Now that everyone is here and you've had time to catch up, it's time to call church so we can figure all this shit out. Blade, call the guys into the chapel." I say as I stand up and put Mina on her own feet. I turn her to me and lay a very possessive kiss on her lips with the Night Howlers looking on.

"Staking your claim Timber?" She asks in a whisper only I can hear.

"You damn straight. It looks like I need all the help I can get at the moment." I whisper back as I look beyond her shoulder into the eyes of Reaper who looks like he's just barely holding himself back from ripping her from my arms.

I give her one last small kiss on her lips. "We'll be done in little bit." I say as all the brothers walk towards the back for church.

An hour later we have gotten Reaper and his crew caught up on everything that has happened so far from the break-in at the shop, the text messages Mina has gotten and the truck exploding.

"I'm pretty sure you all already know who this guy is. So I think its time you tell us everything you know as well." I say to Reaper who is sitting across the table from me.

He let's out a sigh and rubs his face before looking back at me. "His name is Josh. At least we think that is his real name. The last name he gave us turned out to be a fake, so we have no idea who he really is."

"How did you not pick that up on a background check before allowing him into your club?"

"At the time, we had no reason to suspect anything so we didn't dig deeper. If we had, maybe everything could have ended differently. But someone set up the fake name, address, previous employment, all of it, to look legit when we ran his name."

"The week before Mina was attacked is when we realized how wrong we had been to trust him. We had been having a series of break-ins for over a year. Shipments were coming up short and we were losing thousands of dollars at a time. We made the connection early on that it was only happening when Josh was the one that was supposed to be on watch at the storage locations. But we had no proof until that week before. That's when he made a mistake thinking we hadn't installed back-up cameras without telling anyone about it."

"Soon as he realized he'd been caught on camera, he went into hiding. None of us at the time knew he'd been slipping around to see Mina behind our backs and Mina never mentioned it. She always hated the way we intimidated her dates. So I get why she never told us."

"The night of her attack, we'd received word that he'd been spotted in the area but we never thought he'd slip into the house unnoticed and attack her. Grease is the one that heard a noise in the shed and went to see what it was. He pulled Josh off of her and tied him up. Has she told you about that night?" He asks.

"She's told me what she remembers but I have a feeling it's a lot more than that, right?" Feeling my heart beat faster in my chest at the thought of what my girl may have went through in that shed before Grease got to her.

"It was really bad. We aren't sure how many times he hit her in the face but she was so badly beaten that she was unrecognizable. She had multiple fractures and deep bruising to her stomach area. Almost every bone in her hands was broken from her putting up a fight. We know from the doctor that examined her that he didn't rape her but Grease said that when he got into the shed it looked like the son of a bitch was getting ready to rape her from behind."

I could see the anger in Reapers eyes as he retells the story of what happened to Mina. It's the same anger I feel bubbling up inside of me. I can't wait to get my hands on the asshole and teach him why I am named after the wolf. I always get my prey and I tear it apart with my bare hands.

"So what did you do with him? Apparently you didn't kill the fucker as he's now here terrorizing her." Blade asks through clenched teeth.

"That's a damn good question. She is your sister for fucks sake and you let the mother fucker who hurt her live?" Snake asks the group as well.

"We left his ass barely breathing at the bottom of a well in the middle of no where. It's not like we expected that fucker to survive!" Grease growls as he slams his meaty fist on the table.

I can see that this affected their entire club. They all love Mina as a sister and that is clear to see in their eyes. It's her brother Reaper though who seems to be eaten up with guilt.

"Well, what's done is done. None of us can change the past but we can make damn sure that nothing happens to her now or in the future. From the information we have been able to gather so far from all our sources, he is now a part of the Demon Riders.

A local cop we are working with suspects them as the main suspects for some local girls that have come up missing in the last few months. We need to try to find a connection. Something that'll help us to figure out how they are choosing the girls they are taking. Sheriff Wilson is hoping his niece is still alive. We also need to make sure Mina is never alone so that this fucker doesn't get his hands on her."

"I plan to take Mina to a safe location until this is all figured out." Reaper says while looking at me.

"You won't be leaving this compound with Mina." I growl back.

"She's my sister and I plan to make sure she stays safe this time."

"It's not your decision asshole. She is now a part of Wolfsbane." I say as my eyes turn to slits. I really would hate to hurt my girls' brother but I will if he even attempts to take her from me.

"Reaper, he's right. It's not our decision. If Fairy wants to stay, we can not stop her from doing so and I have a feeling she definitely wants to stay." Spark tells his brother in a much calmer voice.

Reaper looks over at his brother for several minutes before he seems to relax and slump back into his seat.

"Fine. I promised Fairy I would try to stop controlling her life so much." He says on a chuckle.

"Can I ask why you all keep calling her Little Fairy?" I ask them all.

"Ha-ha. It's because of how tiny she is. Our father started calling her that the day she was born. It stuck and the whole club calls her that. Seems to fit her personality if you ask me because she was always able to wrap us all around her pretty little pinky finger." Spark tells me while shaking his head as we all move to leave the meeting room.

As we walk into the bar area, I spot Mina on a stool and I feel that tingling feeling in my body that I have felt ever since I first laid eyes on her.

"She definitely has some kind of magic." I say to no one in particular but Reaper hears me as he's standing right next to me.

"I'm pretty sure I do not even want to know." He says shaking his head back and forth. "You have room here for us at the club-house or do we need to find a motel?" He asks.

"There's another building out back with enough rooms for you all. We built it just for visiting MC's several years ago. It's open and should already be stocked with everything you need." I answer.

"Thanks, I appreciate it." He replies as he walks toward the pool tables where his crew is playing a few games and I head towards my girl.

****

Mina

I feel his heat before his arms slip around me from behind and I turn around on my seat to settle my own arms around his waist. He pulls me in close and kisses me gently.

"Mmm, you taste good baby. Like cinnamon. What you been drinking since we were in the back?" He asks with a smile.

"I mentioned to Dane and Fang earlier that I liked Fireball" I say with a shrug. "So they went and picked some up for me."

"Fireball? Can the Little Fairy handle that?" He chuckles.

"You've been asking about my nickname, huh? I can handle it just fine thank you." I say with a smile.

"I also called Bella to come over. She should be here any minute. I want her to meet my brothers. I also owe her an explanation about everything." I say with a blush at the thought of hiding so much for so long.

Timber looks over at the door and says, "Here she is now." I turn and watch her make her way to me and I give her a hug.

"How's the coffee shop?" I ask her.

"It's doing really well as usual. Mom has been taking more shifts to help me out. Ever since the weather started warming up, business has gotten insane. You'd think no one in town knew how to make their own cup of coffee." She says on a laugh.

"So where are these brothers of yours Mina that you've told me so much about?" She asks and I smile at her.

"Come on. They are back by the pool tables. I'll introduce you.

"Reaper, Spark, this is my best friend Bella. Bella these are my brothers. You know Reaper as Rafe and Spark as Matt."

"Nice to meet you all." Bella says.

"It's very nice to finally meet you as well Bella." Spark says with a huge grin as he takes her hand and pulls her into a hug. Blade walks up at the same time and pulls Bella from Spark's arms. She jerks away from him and glares at him while Spark and Blade stare each other down.

"Blade." Timber growls and Blade finally breaks the staring contest he was having with Spark.

We all move to take a seat at a table and again, as before, Bella is left standing without a seat. Spark moves as though he is going to let her have his chair but Blade grabs her and pulls her into his lap. I watch as he whispers to her and she immediately settles down into his lap. Blade looks up at Spark and they each give a chin lift.

"I guess the pissing contest finally has a winner." I whisper giggle to Timber and immediately feel him trying to not laugh out loud as well.

****

Timber

"Come on baby, It's time for bed." I whisper to Mina. For the last 45 minutes she had been dozing on my shoulder while the rest of us sat talking around the table.

She barely opens her eyes to look at me as I stand up with her in my arms and I head down the hall towards our room. I sit her up on the side of the bed and reach to take her clothes and shoes off. Once she's naked, I help her under the covers before taking my own clothes off and slipping in beside her between the sheets.

I pull her close and nuzzle her neck. I can't stop my hands from stroking her body. She's like a drug to me that I can't get out of my system. Not that I even want to anyway. I've waited a long time for a woman like her. My parents always told me that I would know the one meant for me as soon as I set eyes on her. And they were right. Mina is it for me.

Her skin is so smooth as I run my hand across her stomach, making her quiver in response. I continue stroking straight down to her pussy. I have an overwhelming urge to be inside of her, to feel her vice like grip on my cock as I slide in and out of her silky folds.

"Babe, I really need you right now." I say as I rock against her from behind.

"Mmm, I need you too Timber." She whispers back.

I turn her around to face me and lift her leg up over my hip. My hand slides back to her pussy and I plunge two fingers into her. As she gasps, I take her in a deep possessive kiss. Curling my fingers, I bring her to climax quickly. Before she has time for her trimmers to subside, I push my cock into her as deeply as I can. A sense of being home fills my body immediately. She is home to me and I will take care of her until my dying day.

****

Chapter 10

Timber

The next day, I am in the shop doing paperwork when I receive a call from Sheriff Wilson asking for another meeting. They have had another development in the case and he thinks its something important.

"Blade, call all the brothers in, Sheriff Wilson is on the way here with new information."

"Did he say what the information was about, Prez?"

"He didn't say but he sounded like it was really important. Maybe Snake has found something new on all those computers of his."

"I'll go call everyone in and we'll see where we are then. Hopefully we can finally pinpoint exactly where they are hiding out and if they have moved the girls that have been taken further south or across the border recently." Blade says with a disgusted sound to his voice as he walks towards the door.

"Hey, Blade?" I say just before he leaves.

"Yeah?"

"Is everything between you and Bella okay? You seem more distracted lately." I ask.

"I don't know. She drives me crazy, has driven me crazy for years. I'll figure it out. I won't let it keep me from doing my job."

I give him a chin lift in acknowledgement as he leaves the room.

An hour later, all of my guys along with the Night Howlers are standing around the bar waiting for Officer Wilson to arrive. I am truly hoping that with whatever information he has we can locate this other crew quickly and in the process find this Josh guy so I can be sure he never bothers Mina again.

The door finally opens to Officer Wilson and another man that I assume is his deputy.

"Officer Wilson." I say as way of hello.

"Timber. Thanks for seeing us so quickly today."

"Not a problem. Hopefully this helps to locate them quickly and find your niece before anything really bad happens to her. Let's all go into Church and discuss everything." I say as I lead everyone towards our meeting room. My men take their normal seats around the table, while the Night Howlers all stand around the room against the wall. I indicate to Officer Wilson that he should start.

"I asked Timber to meet with me so quickly because we found a camera that picked up what could possibly be the motorcycles that left from my niece's house that night. It at least gives us a direction that they could be headed in. I figured I could bring it to you because I know what your man Snake is capable of. I can't get the judge to give me all the warrants that would be needed for a job this big. So I thought maybe Snake could do his magic and crack into surveillance along the route it seems they were headed in."

"I can definitely see what I can find if you have a starting point. That has been the main issue. I have been trying to watch video from every direction and there are just too many to watch." Snake says as Officer Wilson hands him what information he brought with him and Snake heads towards his computer room. "Give me about 15 minutes." He says just as he leaves the doorway.

"Let's give him his 15 minutes. Everyone go get a drink and as soon as he has something, we'll come back and see where we are."

I head back towards the kitchen where I last seen Mina earlier. I just want to feel her next to me and assure myself that she is still safe. The first thing I notice when I walk in is that she isn't still in there with all the girls and so I head towards our rooms. But she's not in the room or in the bathroom so I head back towards the kitchen to ask the girls if they have seen her.

"Have any of you seen Mina? She's not in our room."

"I think she said something about going to see Bella at the coffee shop." Candy, one of the coyotes answers.

"What? She's not supposed to leave. Why didn't one of you stop her?" I growl back at her.

"Timber, we are club girls; we are not allowed to tell the president's ole lady what she can and can't do. You know that." Candy says while looking scared of my reaction.

"Yeah, I do know that Candy, but one of you could have let a prospect know so that he

129

could stop her. And remind me later to change that stupid ass rule!" I say as I leave the room.

"Reaper!" I yell as I head through the bar area towards the front door causing him to look my way. "Mina left. Supposedly she is headed to see Bella at the coffee shop. Damn woman knew she wasn't supposed to leave! It's not safe!"

"Let's hope she made it okay without any problems. I don't care if she is now your ole lady. I raised that girl even though she is my sister. I plan to tan her hide for this stunt!" He says as he follows me towards our bikes.

****

Mina

My phone started ringing right after Timber walked away with the guys for a meeting in church. I noticed it was Bella's cell number on the display so I stepped outside to answer it.

"Hey chica, what's up at the coffee shop today?"

"Mina?" Bella says back and she sounds like she is frightened.

"Bella? What is wrong? You don't sound right."

"Josh is here. He says for you to meet us in the ally behind the coffee shop in 15 minutes. If you don't, he will rape and kill me." She says as she busts into tears.

"Tell that bastard that I am coming. I'm leaving right now Bella. Don't worry."

"He says to tell you that you had better be alone or he will shoot me in the head and still get away."

"I swear. I will tell no one. I am grabbing my purse and headed your way. Stay strong Bella. I love you!"

Her phone clicks off before she is able to say anything else. I have got to hurry. I don't know exactly how I am going to get past the prospects without them letting Timber know but I have to try. Bella is in this mess because of me.

Walk slowly back through the kitchen. One of the girls asks where I am going and I do mention the coffee shop but I know that she won't stop me. The club girls are not allowed to say anything to the president's ole lady. I figure mentioning the coffee shop will still alert Timber that something is up but will allow me a head start so that Josh doesn't know that I am being followed.

I pull up to the back entrance of the coffee shop about ten minutes later. There is a dark colored van with tinted windows and I watch the driver side door open to reveal Josh, the asshole I haven't seen since the night of my party. Chill bumps break out across my arms and the hair on the back of my neck stands up. I am scared but I remind myself that I am not the same girl that this bastard used to know. He walks towards me as I step out of the rental car the insurance company provided for my use even though I haven't been using it until today.

"My dear, sweet little Fairy." He says with a huge smile on his face like he is greeting a really old friend.

"I am NOT your Fairy, you bastard! Where is Bella?" I demand to know.

"Now that isn't the way you should speak to me Mina. I'd suggest you be a bit nicer or I may have to teach you another lesson that you didn't learn the last time."

He grabs me by the arm to drag me to him and slams his mouth down on mine. I immediately begin to fight him off and he steps back before slapping me across the face. Pain erupts across my cheek bone and I can feel my left eye beginning to swell immediately.

"I said to behave Mina. Don't make me mark up your beautiful face." He says as he pets the side of my face that he just slapped.

"Please Josh, where is Bella?" I ask in a more calm voice.

"You will see Bella here directly."

"You aren't going to let her go?"

"I never said that I would little Fairy. I only said that I wouldn't kill her if you came to me as I asked. Now I am telling you that if you don't play nice, I will torture her in front of you until you learn your place. And make no mistake Mina, your place is on the floor at my feet, doing whatever I tell you to do." He says as he shoves me into the back of the van.

I hear laughter as I land in the back. As I look around I see a couple other guys that are clearly part of another motorcycle club.

"She's cute boss-man." One says to Josh as he gets into the driver seat.

"Just keep your fucking hands off. She is mine! I will shoot any of you bastards if you think otherwise." He responds back to them.

The van starts moving but I don't know in what direction we are headed in. I can only hope that Timber notices that I am gone and gets on the hunt quickly to find me. Hopefully by then I know where to find Bella so that we can get her out of this mess in one piece as well. I just that she forgives me for all of this. Every bit of it is my fault.

****

Timber

We pull up to *Bella's Brew* but do not see any cars parked out front and the closed sign is on the front door.

"It doesn't look like they are here." Reaper says.

"There's a back parking lot. Let's check there before we leave. I'm getting a bad feeling about this." I say as we start walking towards the back.

I immediately see the car Mina left in sitting by the back door. Looking inside we spot her purse still sitting in the passenger seat but her cell phone appears to not be inside. That can help us to trace her movements so I send a text off to Snake and explain to him what is going on.

"I have Snake looking into tracing her and Bella's phones and looking at the surveillance cameras in the area. He should have something for us in a couple minutes. Christ! We have to assume that Bella has been taken as well, which means I am going to have one pissed off brother showing up in a few minutes." I finish saying as we immediately begin to hear motorcycle engines getting closer.

Blade pulls into the back lot along with some of the other brothers and also some of the brothers from the Night Howlers.

"Bella?" Blade asks in way of a question and I just shake my head no. I can see the fear and anger as it rolls through his body. His hands clinch the handles of his bike as he struggles to get control of himself. I know how he's feeling. There is nothing to compare to the fury running through my bones. This fucker and all who helped him will die painful deaths.

My phone finally pings with a text from Snake.

"Bella's phone is showing a location in the mountain just north of here and Mina's phone is on the move in the same direction. I asked Snake to get us aerial photos of the area that Bella's phone is located and he says he should have a picture of the guy that took Mina in a few minutes."

"Should we get Officer Wilson in on this?" asks Reaper.

"We should probably wait and see what we find when we get there. These may not even be the same guys that have been taking the girls and even if they are, the girls may not be in the same area with Mina and Bella." says Blade.

"Blade is right. I want to be absolutely sure of what we are dealing with here. Don't want to lose any of our men by rushing in without a plan in place." I say to all the guys as they shake their heads in agreement.

"Let's get back to the clubhouse and strap up. I'll get Spark to gather what he needs. I have a feeling that we will need to blow shit up tonight." Reaper says as we head back to our bikes.

Chapter 11

Mina

They blind folded me before we arrived to wherever the hell we are now. Pretty sure I heard us move through a couple gates before they opened the van door to drag me out. At least the bastard that carried me in untied my hands before slamming the door shut and locking it.

My phone is still in my boot where I slipped it before coming face to face with Josh. Stupid pricks didn't even bother checking to see if I had anything on me. I might have been naïve when I was young but my family didn't raise a fool. They taught me from an early age of what to do in these types of situations. Just wish I could check the time without them finding it.

As soon as I have that thought, I hear the door being unlocked and pushed open. Josh walks in with a paper bag in his hand.

"I have supper for you my love. It's not much, just a sandwich and some chips, got you a sprite to wash it down with, too." He smiles at me as if this was a normal situation.

"Josh, you know that this isn't going to end well for you. My brothers will find you and this time they will kill you."

"If that is true Mina, I will make sure that you die right next to me where you belong." He looks around the sparse room before his eyes return to me. "This will be our room tonight. Are there enough blankets on the bed?"

"Josh, I will not willingly sleep in this room with you."

"You won't have a choice Mina. Tonight, I take what should have always been mine. I'll be back in a little while. I need to check on everything before bed." He says as he walks out of the door.

This man has lost all his marbles! I think to myself. There is no way I will submit to him. He will have to kill me first. I plan to fight!!

****

Timber

By the time we reach the clubhouse, Snake has all the information we need on the location where Mina and Bella were taken to. It looks like a lot of old abandoned buildings and the newest satellite images show only a hand full of vehicles there at any given time over the past couple weeks.

"I don't think these are the assholes kidnapping girls." Blade says while looking over my shoulder.

"I don't think it is either but let's be sure we clear all the buildings from top to bottom. I want to make sure we don't overlook anything that might possibly help to find them as well." I say to all the men gathered around me.

"I will double check to be sure who the enemy is before I light anything up." Spark comments.

"Please do because I don't want an episode like last time where I almost lost the family jewels." Laughs Reaper, while cupping said jewels.

"We all know the only family jewel in this family is Mina. We definitely don't need any mini Reapers running around. No telling who'd they kill off in preschool!"

After everyone has a little laugh at the banter between the brothers, everyone seems to get more serious and begins to strap up with weapons. Spark seems to have a lot of homemade explosives. I have absolutely no idea how he rigged them up so quickly.

I've heard a lot of rumors about the brothers over the years. They are known to be extremely dangerous and deadly. It's told that Spark likes to watch grown men as he blows them up with his homemade bombs but not before he watches their faces melt from the acid he always seems to have at hand.

As for Reaper, it is said that he is an expert at skinning a man alive and then torturing them, if they are still alive to be tortured, by slowly dripping alcohol on the exposed meat.

Not that I am judging them. I know exactly what I am known for and this asshole Josh will find out exactly what that is before the life leaves his eyes.

"Are we ready to ride?" I ask looking around at the group of men dressed for battle. Everyone nods as we head towards our bikes.

I can't stop to think about what Mina might have already suffered or is currently suffering. It will make me act reckless and I can't afford to be reckless with her life. All I want in my head at the moment are thoughts of destroying every man found in those abandoned buildings. They will all die, that is a certainty.

"Let's ride!" I yell to all the men as we start all the bikes at once.

****

Mina

An hour passes as I wait to see what Josh will do next or hopefully be saved from this nightmare. No one will tell me where Bella is or even if she is close by. I don't even know if she is located in this building. I can only hear some of the men talking as they come close to my door otherwise I can't hear anything outside of this room.

I am in the middle of trying this small window that I know that not even I can fit through when the door behind me opens.

"There's no need to be scared of our wedding night Little Fairy." Josh says when he sees me trying the window.

"We aren't married you stupid sick bastard. What the hell are you even talking about?"

"We were bound together in blood that night. Don't you remember?"

As I give him what I know is a horrified stare, he shrugs his shoulders.

"I might have hit your head too hard on the table. But it doesn't matter. All that matters is we were bound by blood in the old rituals passed down through my family from New Orleans."

"Dear God, you really are off your rocker aren't you? You need some serious help Josh. I don't know what I thought I ever saw in you. I do know that it damn sure wasn't love. We are NOT married. You will have to kill me tonight because I will not willingly submit to you." I say more calmly than I feel. It's as if I am truly tired and just ready for fate to take over, wherever that may lead.

He stares at me for a few minutes and then quicker than I can blink, he is on me. I get one good hit into his face before he hits me in the temple and my vision goes dark. I can feel him drag me to the bed and begin to tie me down. The whole time he is rubbing his body against mine like a sick fucking cat and all I want to do is throw up.

"You can't get a willing woman so you resort to tying one up. Bless your heart." I mumble through the swelling of my lips just before he hits me again. Right when I feel him start to mess with my jeans, there's a loud boom and the room starts to shake.

"Mother fucker!!" screams Josh as he jumps up and runs out of the door.

I'm left alone at last. I don't know what that sound was but I am really hoping that it was my brother Spark. He certainly loves to blow shit up.

I try to get my hands loose and I can feel the ropes biting into my wrists. I can hear gunshots outside and more load booms that seem to be getting closer to where I am. If it's Timber and my brothers out there, I pray that they also find poor Bella.

****

Timber

We cut the engines about a mile before the abandoned buildings so that we won't be heard and walk the rest of the way in. We can tell that there isn't much for security around the place. The two that were supposed to be guards we took out very easily with a slit to the throat.

"Spark, go do what you do. Everyone else, spread out, check buildings as you go and take out every mother fucker you come across. Except that fucker Josh, I want him alive to suffer the fate he has coming to him." I tell the men as we set out to find the girls.

Blade stays right next to me as we clear buildings and take out the trash. I can feel his anxiety and anger over Bella as we go.

"Don't worry Blade, we will find her."

"I really hope so Timber. I can't lose her without her ever knowing what she means to me. I never got a chance to tell her."

"Don't worry; you'll get your chance."

We hear the first of Spark's bombs go off and then all hell breaks lose with the gunfire all around us. I take out about four more of the bastards before I spot a building that wasn't on the aerial photos we got from Snake.

"Blade, that building back there wasn't on our Intel. I bet that is exactly where we will find the girls and Josh too."

"Let's go. But you might want to call it in over to Spark and Reaper so they can make their way over there as well." He says as we hunker down behind some shipping containers.

"Spark, there's a building in the very back that didn't show up in our aerials. I'm betting that is where we will find them."

"I can see it from here. We will meet you there in less than two minutes." He replies back over the radio.

"They will meet us at the door. Let's go." I say to Blade.

As we come up to the building on one side, Reaper and Spark come up from the other.

"I think our men have taken out most of the fuckers out here." Reaper says.

"Good. One thing before we go in here. I know that you want your vengeance on this fucker for what he's done. She's your sister but she is also my ole lady. You can get your turn at him but keep him alive because I get to end the life that is left." I say to them both. They finally nod their heads at me and we head into the building.

The first door opens up into a larger room and right in the middle we see Josh. He is sitting in the middle of a pattern on the floor that looks like it was drawn with blood and he's chanting a bunch of words that I can't make out. He is completely naked as he picks up a bottle and begins to pour what's inside on himself.

"What the fuck?" Reaper says as we all watch the crazy bastard in the middle of the room.

"You are too late now. I have taken my brides." Josh calmly states when he finally looks up and notices us.

"Where are the girls?" I ask him.

"Around." He answers as he begins to laugh in a maniacal way.

"Blade, check the rooms on the right. Reaper and I will check on the left while Spark keeps an eye on this crazy fuck."

The first couple rooms are completely empty. Its when Reaper opens the fourth door that my heart speeds up at the sight in front of me. On a table in the middle of the room is a completely naked Bella. She is covered in blood and bruise.

"Oh fuck! BLADE!!" I scream as I run over to check her pulse.

Blade rushes in behind me as I am covering her with an old sheet I found in the floor.

"Mother fuck! What the hell did he do to her?"

"I don't know but she does still have a pulse. Get a cage and get her to the hospital. Also call Officer Wilson. We'll need his help if any questions are asked at the hospital." Reaper and I watch as Blade carries the woman he loves from the room.

"Reaper, let's get the rest of the rooms checked." I can tell that he has the same fears as I do at the moment about Mina.

After a complete search of the building, we still hadn't found Mina. Reaper and Spark had already began beating on Josh trying to get the fucker to break and tell us where he has her locked up. It doesn't seem to be working as the more punches they delivered; the more laughter seems to be the only thing coming out of his mouth.

All the other guys that were sweeping the rest of the compound had started to trickle in from outside to watch the beating.

"Enough! I want everyone to spread out and do another search. Do it quietly while everyone yells her name. Hopefully she'll hear one of us and yell back so that we can find her. She has to be here somewhere. Now find my woman damn it!" I tell all the guys as my anger and anxiety begins to take over. I'm more than ready to snap this bastard's neck but not before I find my girl.

Everyone spreads out quickly and quietly as I asked them to do. Every so often you can hear one of them call Mina's name. This goes on for more than thirty minutes before one of the brother's on the far side of the compound sends word that he heard something through a door that looks like it leads to a basement. I get over there quickly and as I am walking up he tells me that the door was so well hidden, it must have been overlooked by whoever swept the area.

"Looks like the lock may be rigged with an explosive. That is your expertise Spark. Come see what you can do with it."

"Yeah, I'll have this off in 2 minutes." Spark replies.

I stand behind him as patiently as I can and true to his word, in less than 2 minutes the door is open.

I slowly push the door open and there, tied on the bed is my girl. Other than a few bruises to her face, she appears to be okay.

"Mina!" I say, crossing the room to her.

"Thank God Timber. I didn't know if y'all would make it in time. Please tell me y'all found Bella in this hell hole? I haven't seen her and he wouldn't tell me where she was."

"We found her baby, stop worrying. Blade took her to the hospital. She was breathing but she looked like she was in pretty bad shape." I answer as I untie her from the ropes and she jumps into my arms.

"Let's go have you checked out at the hospital my Little Fairy. We will check on Bella while we are there."

As we walk out, I give orders for the crazy bastard to be taken to our basement at the clubhouse. The guys and I will deal with him later.

Chapter 12

Mina

"We've been here for over an hour Timber, I need to go check on Bella!"

I was beginning to get frustrated with Timber and the Doctor. They refuse to let me out of the room until every test they could possibly think of is run.

"We will check on Bella as soon as the Doctor comes back with your results! You heard him say that the bones in your cheek under your eye could possibly be fractured. Can't you just understand that we need to be sure that you are okay first?" He says with a sigh in his voice.

I completely understand where he's coming from but damn it, I have been poked and prodded the entire hour I have been here. The most they have found of course is the bones in my cheek, which is exactly the only place I told them that I could possibly be hurt at.

"Honey, can you at least stick your head out the door and yell at them to get a move on?" I say as I start to bat my eyes at him. I'm sure I look ridiculous as one of my eyes is swollen shut.

He shakes his head at me with a smile, "Sure baby. I'll intimidate the nurses and see what is going on."

He heads out of the room and I hear him talking to the nurses that are at their desks in the hall. I could try to make a break for it but I know that I won't get very far. There's no way that Timber wouldn't see me leave this room. Besides, I am pretty sure that my brothers are out there somewhere as well.

"Boy, being surrounded by a bunch of boys can suck sometimes." I whisper to myself.

"I heard that." Timber says as he walks back into the room.

"Did you find out anything?"

"Yes, there doesn't seem to be any fractures, just badly bruised. They wrote you a couple prescriptions for pain and swelling."

"Can we go find out about Bella now?"

"Yes sweetheart, come on. Blade sent me a message saying they are in a room down the hall."

I quickly follow Timber out of the room. If I had stepped outside in the hall, I would have known which room Bella was in by the pissed off Blade standing outside the door. It looks like my best friend may have thrown him out of the room and barred him entry.

"Go ahead in with Bella, I'm going to talk to Blade for a few minutes." Timber says as he kisses my cheek and opens the door for me.

I am not prepared for the sight that is in front of me as I walk into the room. My eyes immediately fill with tears and I watch her turn towards the sound of my footsteps coming towards her.

"No need to cry Mina. I'll survive. It's just a lot of bruising and I lost a lot of blood. At least

I'm awake now. Is Blade still in the hall?" she asks.

"Yes and he looks like he's in hell. Did you throw him out of the room?"

"Yes, I did and I don't want to talk about it."

"We don't have to talk about it right now. What did the doctor say?"

"He said I'd be in here for a day or two for observation, then he'd let me go home."

I can tell from the way she's avoiding eye contact that she isn't telling me something but I don't want to push her right now. I take a chair next to her bed so that I can hold her hand. Whatever she is not telling me, I can clearly see is hurting her very badly. It's not physical but something deeply emotional.

****

Timber

"What's going on man? Why are you out here in the hall instead of with Bella?" I ask Blade as soon as the door shuts behind Mina.

"I don't want to talk about it right now." He says through clenched teeth. "That mother fucker in the basement?" He asks with fire in his eyes.

"Yeah, the other brothers took him there while I brought Mina to the hospital."

"How is she anyway? I mean I know I just seen her but how's that bruise on her cheek?"

"Doc said it was just a deep bruise and would heal completely. She got lucky."

"Yeah, she did." He says as he stares off down the hall for a minute. "I get my shot with that bastard, you understand?"

"Perfectly brother, I understand perfectly." I say as I look him directly in the eyes. "What does the doc say about Bella?"

"She'll heal. You think Mina would stay with her while we head back to the club to take care of shit?" I can see the rage that he is just barely holding inside.

"Yeah brother, I want the shit taken care of before the girls leave the hospital. Let me tell Mina where we are going and we can head out. You want to say bye to Bella?" I ask as I start to open the door.

"Nah, she doesn't want me in the room right now." He says on a sigh. "But no worries, once this is dealt with, she will definitely be seeing a lot of me. She just needs to get used to the idea." He says as he heads down the hall. I guess he will get around to telling me what is going on eventually.

When I walk into the hospital room, Bella is sleeping and Mina is just sitting in the chair watching her. I lean down to whisper to her so that I don't wake up Bella.

"Baby, me and the boys got to go take care of a few things. We may be gone a few hours. Can you stay with Bella until we get back?"

"Yeah honey. I think there's more going on with her than just all of this anyway. I want to be here for her in case she wants to talk about it."

"I got that same feeling from Blade a few minutes ago out in the hall."

"He tell you anything?"

"Not a word but it'll all work out eventually."

"You're right." She reaches up and kisses me on the cheek and looks right in my eyes. "Be careful honey, okay?"

"You know it babe. I love you, ya know?" I say to her for the first time. I know that I should have already let her know how I felt about her. I'm not always upfront in my feelings like a woman needs from a man.

"I know you do. I love you completely too." She says back and I can't stop myself from giving her a deep kiss that says everything.

****

We get back to the clubhouse about forty five minutes after leaving the hospital. Officer Wilson had to talk to me before we could leave so that we had the story straight on what happened out at the warehouses. I head straight towards the basement with the rest of the guys.

"Before we head in here I have a few things I want to say. I know we all want a piece of this asshole for what he has done but I get his final moments. Are we clear?" I say to Blade and Mina's brothers.

Reaper and Spark look at each other a minute before answering me. "We are cool with that but he gets a taste of what we have for him." Reaper says and I give him a chin lift before looking over at Blade.

"I plan to be there for those final moments Timber. This became extremely personal when he did what he did to Bella."

"You ready to tell me everything that you haven't told me yet? I know there's more than what you said to me at the hospital."

"No, I'm not but I promise I'll tell you brother soon as I get my head wrapped around it."

"Fair enough, let's get this over with." I say as I open the door to the basement and we walk in.

Josh is hanging from the ceiling by a chain. All the tools are laid out and ready to be used as I had asked the brothers to do before I got here. The fucker raises his head as we come into the room. He looks like a few of the brothers had a little fun with him before we got here.

"Joshy, Joshy, Joshy….." Reaper says as he circles around him. "You are about to get exactly what you should have gotten years ago. Are you ready? I even brought my sweet babies with me just for you."

Reaper walks over to the table with all the knives and picks up a bag that clearly belongs to him as it has a Reaper holding a head on the side of it. Looks like I will finally see the famous Reaper in action and I although I have seen and done some things, I am not sure if I can handle watching what I know is about to happen.

He pulls out this wicked looking filet knife that was clearly specially made. You can tell by the look of it that it is extremely sharp and has a curved end on it. It is also stamped with the name Reaper on the blade. He doesn't say another word as he walks over to Josh and a quick flick of the wrist he has cut his left nipple off. Josh immediately begins to scream.

****

Mina

Bella wakes up every so often from nightmares. The nurses come and go bringing her medication to help her sleep. I keep a close watch on her as I sit in the chair beside her bed. I had been sitting with her for three hours when she opens her eyes and slowly looks over at me then begins to cry softly.

"Oh sweetie, it's okay, you are safe now." I say as I begin to wipe her tears.

"It's not Mina."

"Sure it is. You'll be better in no time and back to your normal self."

"No. You don't understand. You can't possibly understand." She moans and begins crying huge sobs that shake the whole bed. I don't know what she is talking about. All I can do is hold her close as she cries herself back to sleep.

Several hours later, Timber comes to take me home and I leave Bella with Blade by her side. She was still asleep when I left. I can only hope and pray my sweet friend can get through this without it causing her to end our friendship.

"I hope Bella gets better quickly." I say to Timber as we lay in bed.

"I'm sure it'll take time. She has Blade to help her through it. She may not know it yet, hell, he probably hasn't even told her, but he loves her. He'd do anything for her."

"I hope you are right. I feel like this is my entire fault."

"Stop blaming yourself Mina. You couldn't control that crazy bastard and his actions."

"What happened to him anyway?"

"You don't worry about any of that my Little Fairy. Just know he'll never be a bother to anyone ever again."

"One of those, club business and can't tell me kinda things?" I ask him straight out.

"Exactly, my love, you were raised in this. You know how it all goes down. Now tell me you'll marry me next month and make everything official."

I can do nothing but gasp before he starts kissing me. So I convey my answer in my kiss as best that I can. Once he finally let's me up for air, he asks, "That's a yes right?"

"Yes, honey, that is a definite yes!"

The end.
More from the Wolfsbane Ridge MC coming soon.
Continue for a sneak peek of Blade and Bella's story.

Blade's Pixie

Chapter 1

Blade

I have been in love with Bella Winters for years. There was only one problem; she wouldn't give me the time of day. At least she wouldn't until recently. We finally hooked up one night and I thought that it was a foregone conclusion that we were an item. But according to her hardheaded ass, it didn't mean shit. Even though our one night together resulted in consequences that I had no idea about until it was too late.

Ever since she was attacked, she hasn't allowed me close to her. It doesn't keep me from doing some stalker type shit such as sleeping on her front step and constantly having her watched by one of the prospects. She hasn't said anything directly to me about it but according to Fang she let him know real quick that she didn't appreciate any of it.

"Damn woman." I mumble under my breath as I head into the clubhouse to speak to my best friend and president, Timber.

When I reach his office, he is on the phone and doesn't sound too happy about whatever it is he is hearing. So I take a seat at his desk to wait, which doesn't take too long as he plops down into his own seat with a sigh.

"Problems Prez?"

"That was Officer Wilson on the phone. They found evidence at the warehouses that suggests the kidnapped girls were transported to Louisiana. They may be in the same position that Bella found herself in." He says with raised brows.

"Fuck!" I say as I shake my head at the image. "What are we going to do Prez?"

"I think I should call my future in laws and get them in on this since it is located in their territory. They have more contacts there that could dig up information that likes to remain hidden from outsiders."

"That's a good idea."

"I also think I will send you out to give them some help."

"I can't leave Bella right now Prez! Fuck! I just nearly lost her. Actually, she's further away from me now than she's ever fucking been!"

"You both need time Blade! And you ARE fucking going! I'll keep an eye on Bella. Every brother here will and you know it. She may be saying she's not yours but everyone in town knows better. It'll do you good to get away and clear your head. Go help out on this missing girl's case. When you come back, Bella and you both will be more settled with a clear head."

I know that Timber means well and there is probably some truth in what he says, but I seriously don't want to leave Bella right now.

Far as I know, no one yet knows about the baby. The baby we both lost.

"Okay, Prez, I'll go but only because you are making me. Just let me tell Bella that I am going. And for the love of God make sure she stays safe!"

"You can count on it brother. Officer Wilson will be going out with you in his own truck. He's taking some personal leave from the sheriff's office. I think it was pushed on him by the Mayor because of how close to the case he is. They know he's going to Louisiana but he's been ordered to turn everything in that he finds out into the fed's."

"Well, fucking hell!! You mean I got to watch out for those bastards while out there too? Come on Timber, this is getting even more fucked up!"

"I know that it is but I have a firm suspicion that Reaper can help out with the fed's. His MC has been in that territory for a really long time and with that comes connections that we will need."

"I'll head out in an hour after I talk to Bella. Or I should say, try to talk to Bella."

"She still won't speak to you?"

"Not a peep since the night we rescued her and Mina." I sigh and rub my neck as I can feel a headache coming on. "I'll call you as soon as I get there and check up as often as possible. Keep me updated on Bella. I have a feeling she's gearing up to act out as soon as I am out of sight."

"You know I will Blade. Good luck out there and if you need anything, call me. I can be out as soon as possible." Timber says as he shakes my hand and I walk out the door headed to see the one girl I love that refuses to love me back.

****
Bella

I can hear the motorcycle way before I can see it. I know exactly who it is. I haven't spoken one word to him since I told him about the baby that night. I know he blames me, I could tell by the way he shut down on me as soon as he found out. He left the room and didn't come back for hours. He claims he loves me but if he did, he wouldn't have left me in my grief.

I don't look up as I hear him coming up the front steps but I can see the toes of his boots.

"How are you doing Bella?" He asks but I continue to stare at the toes of his boots. He let's out a long sigh.

"Fine, you don't have to talk, just listen. I'm going out of town for awhile. Not sure exactly how long I will be gone but when I come back we are working this shit out. I'm more than tired of the silent treatment."

I try not to react to his words, although it is like a knife to the heart. How can he run off like this after everything we have been through? What I have been through?

"I'll call and text you every day. I really hope you answer because I will miss you *Pixie.* I love you so very much; I have for a really long time."

"STOP!! Just stop saying you love me Blade! I am sick of hearing you lie to me!! Just run off to God knows where and leave me the hell alone!" I scream at him as I run inside.

A few minutes later I can hear the sound of his engine as he roars away. I am sure in that moment that everyone in the county can hear the sound as my heart breaks into a billion pieces.

I hope you enjoyed the sneak peek of *Blade's Pixie.* **Please check back for a future publication date.**

About the Author;

Marissa Ann lives in a very small southern town in North Mississippi with her youngest 3 children and her favorite pit-bull dog named, Blues Man. She has two grandbabies that she adores and spends as much time with as she can get. She has always enjoyed reading anything and everything she can. She loves hearing from her readers and other author's, so look her up on Facebook or send her a message at <u>marissaann2018@yahoo.com</u>

"I don't teach my children that "the sky is the limit". Absolutely not! That suggests that there is a limit. I teach them to reach for the galaxies…" – Marissa Ann